Praise for TOM DRURY

'A major figure in American literature, author of a string of novels without a dud in the bunch . . . Drury gives us the wondrous and engaging stuff of real storytelling.' NEW YORK TIMES

'Drury is a big-time American talent' JONATHAN FRANZEN

'Tom Drury's spooky neo-noir novel proves there is no one better at tangling up the lives of small Midwestern weirdos' VANITY FAIR on *The Driftless Area*

'Drury is enormously skilled . . . this fine novel ends with a tug-of-war between the spiritual we don't altogether trust and the grind we're somehow unable to resist' NEW YORK TIMES on *The Driftless Area*

'A near-masterpiece . . . Drury imbues the landscape with an impersonal, threatening and ancient chill . . . reminiscent of Twin Peaks –a hypnotic and memorable read' TIME OUT on *The Driftless Area*

'This is fiction that doesn't thrust its greatness upon you so much as insinuate itself through vivid, credible characters, close observation, and lovely, deadpan dialogue . . . *The End of Vandalism* is a masterpiece.' INDEPENDENT ON SUNDAY

'takes you to wonderful places, and spins a fine narrative from the apparent mundanity of lives being lived' GUARDIAN on *The End of Vandalism*

'If you read *The End of Vandalism* you will become one of those people who try to foist it upon other people, your eyes shining with the unsettling delight of having lived through it.' JON MCGREGOR

'The always fresh perspective o'
have you responding like his ch
prise in her heart".' KIRKUS RE

THE
DRIFTLESS
AREA

TOM DRURY

Old Street Publishing

Published in Great Britain in 2015 by Old Street Publishing Ltd
Yowlestone House, Devon EX16 8LN
www.oldstreetpublishing.co.uk

ISBN 978-1-910400-11-1

The right of Tom Drury to be identified as the author of this work has been asserted by him in
accordance with the Copyright, Designs and Patents Act 1988.

10 9 8 7 6 5 4 3 2 1

A CIP catalogue record for this title is available from the British Library.

Printed and bound in Great Britain by CPI Group (UK) Ltd, Croydon, CR0 4YY.

TO CLAUDIA

ACKNOWLEDGMENTS

The author would like to thank Elisabeth Schmitz and Sarah Chalfant.

Just prior to this a daughter of the prosperous Chang family, named Yen-erh, died at the age of fifteen suddenly without any apparent cause. In the night, however, she came to life again, stood up, and wished to hasten out; the family barred the door and would not hear of her doing so. Thereupon she said: "I am the spirit of the daughter of a subprefect.... Really I am a ghost, so what is the use of confining me here?"

—*Strange Stories from the Liao Chai*

ONE

THEIR NAMES were Pierre Hunter and Rebecca Lee, and they were seventeen years old, and he had come to see her in the hospital, because she had got pneumonia after running in a cross-country match on a rainy weekend.

She lay in the bed, holding the rails with pale and slender hands, and said it had to be dark in the room or she could not sleep.

"This is not darkness," she said. "The light comes in all night."

"Maybe keep the blinds drawn."

"I do. I'm talking about when they're drawn."

Pierre walked over and looked out the window. The parking lot was lit by a grid of streetlamps, one of which stood just outside the glass. And the light it gave was white with a blue center.

"I see what you mean," he said. "It's sort of like arc welding."

"You should be here later, when the lights are out in the room," she said. "As bad as it is now, it's worse then. And it makes a humming sound, which I don't like either."

"Yeah. I don't hear that."

She ran her fingers through her hair, which was short and brown with red streaks and sharp tufts like sideburns.

"Well," she said, "it's not doing it now."

"Did you talk to somebody?"

"They gave me this."

She opened a drawer in the night table and tossed him a black eye mask with an elastic strap.

"To wear on my head," she said. "Do you believe it? Who could sleep with that on their eyes?"

"Probably some people can," said Pierre.

"Not this one."

"Otherwise they wouldn't make them."

"Just tell them to shut it off, okay?"

When it was time to leave, Pierre went to see the nurse in charge of the floor. She nodded in a rapid tremor and looked beyond him, as if she had written off in advance whatever he might have to say.

"Rebecca is heavily medicated," she said. "She doesn't always know what's going on. She's sleeping. You don't have to worry about that."

"There's this light."

"Oh, yes. The light she talks about."

"Well, I mean, there *is* a light."

"Of course there is a light."

"And it makes a noise."

"There are lots of lights," said the nurse. "It's a hospital. I imagine we would have a few lights and noises. And it would be a very dark hospital indeed if we start shutting lights off for no more reason than this."

They talked or argued for a while longer. Pierre figured that the nurse was the sort of person who always dealt with requests by saying they were impossible, even if they weren't or she had no idea.

But on the next night, three lights in the parking lot did go out, including the one outside Rebecca's window.

Sent to investigate, an electrician from the hospital found that a circuit breaker had tripped in a locked box on a ramp behind the Dumpsters.

This was a little odd but it happened from time to time, and the electrician reset the switch, and the lights came on, and he thought no more about it until the next night, when the same three lights were out again, and again he turned them on.

On the third night the electrician got a thermos of coffee and waited in his truck in the parking lot. Around ten o'clock he saw someone in a hooded sweatshirt leave the hospital, walk up the ramp, open the breaker box, and turn off the lights.

The electrician capped the thermos and stepped down from the truck. Cleverly, he did not call out or make noise, and he almost caught up with the tall hooded figure without a chase. But not quite. There was a chase, and the electrician was not a fast runner, and the one who put out the lights would have got away except that he made the mistake of veering into the hospital gardens, which were in a courtyard with no other way out. There the electrician caught him by the arm and pulled the hood back and saw that it was only a kid.

"Not so fast, you," he said. "What's your name?"

"Pierre Hunter," said Pierre. "My girlfriend's on the third floor. She can't sleep because of the lights."

"Let me tell you something," said the electrician. "Tampering with hospital electricity is not only illegal, it's dangerous. You could cut somebody's life support off. Did you ever think of that?"

"As if they would run the power for something like that through the parking lot," said Pierre.

"Oh, you're a wiring expert now."

"And there's a diagram inside the cover."

"Yes, quite," said the electrician. "I drew it. But tell me this. How are you opening the lock?"

"The combination's on the back," said Pierre.

They went to the breaker box, where the electrician saw that it was true.

"Kind of defeats the purpose," he said.

He reset the circuit, but as chance would have it, while two of the lights came on and stayed on, the third flared and burned out.

"Is that the one?" said the electrician.

"I think it is."

"I guess she'll sleep okay tonight."

What Pierre had done could have been interpreted as a misguided attempt to override an uncaring bureaucracy, and the hospital knew this. Rebecca Lee was not the only one who had complained about the lights and the sound they made.

So instead of going to the police, the chief of security just told Pierre to stay out of the hospital. And the parking lot too.

One night during Pierre's banishment from the hospital grounds, a friend of Rebecca's named Carrie Sloan came to the Hunter place, above the town of Shale, where Pierre lived in a big house on three acres with his mother and father and their dog, a Labrador retriever named Monster.

Pierre had been out in the yard listening to the owls in the hemlocks, and now he and Carrie talked in the garage by the Sabre mowers.

"Listen, Rebecca's breaking up with you," said Carrie. "She wanted you to be the first to know."

"Oh, good," said Pierre.

"Sorry."

"But you knew before I did."

"Well, you're *among* the first."

"She could have called."

"She can't deal with the phone right now, Pierre."

"Have somebody dial and hold the receiver."

"Is the phone the real issue?" said Carrie Sloan. "Probably not, right? Of course it must be painful and everything."

"It's not because of the light."

"No. She's forgotten all about that. There is no why, Pierre. It is what it is."

"What does that mean?"

"Think about it."

"Of course it is what it is. If it wasn't, it wouldn't be."

"Well, it's a very popular thing to say."

"I guess it means 'Too damned bad, ain't it.'"

"If that's what you want it to mean," she agreed.

"Even before she got sick I couldn't tell if she wanted to go with me anymore."

"Well, now you know. She doesn't."

"Have her write me a letter."

"I'll pass along your request but I can't make any

promises." Turning toward a white MGA in the garage, she asked, "Is that your car?"

"I can drive it," said Pierre. "It's not mine per se."

They stood and looked at the two-seat convertible. The tense curve of the back fenders gave way to a long sweep of side panels, and the grill reclined sharply between eager round headlamps.

"Let's go for a spin," said Carrie.

"Okay, jump in."

Pierre revved the MGA and bolted up to the power station that some called Frankenstein's Playground and parked at the chain link gate. They hardly talked along the way because the ride took only a few minutes.

"It's beautiful, isn't it," said Pierre.

She laid her long arm on the door of the car and smiled crookedly, as if she had him all figured out despite not really caring if she figured him out or not.

She was famous for this smile in high school.

"Is this your idea of a funny place to take me?" she said.

"Sort of, yeah."

"You're mad at me for bearing the message."

"It's the way you bear it," said Pierre. "You're obviously getting into it."

"So, is your heart broken or what? Are you crying? I hope you're not crying."

"Just on the inside."

"Do you ever say anything serious?"

"Sometimes, sure," Pierre admitted. "You know what the guy said to me when he caught me putting out the lights? 'Yes, quite.' Isn't that strange? Could he be English?"

"I don't know," said Carrie. "Anyone *could* be English."

"That's true."

"If they're from England."

"Yes, that would decide it."

Carrie was captain of the poetry team, and she said that she had written a poem about Rebecca at the track meet where she caught pneumonia.

"Let's hear it," said Pierre.

> *Oak leaves ladle rain on the runners in the rain*
> *And we wait for Rebecca in vain.*
> *Like a horse hemmed in by the herd*
> *She can't get free to lead.*
> *Something isn't right—it's plain—*
> *Because she excels on this terrain.*

"That's good," said Pierre.

"But what."

"Oh, nothing."

"No, no, that's all right. I hear some hesitation there."

"Well, it kind of goes in and out as far as rhyming, but I guess you can do that."

She nodded. "Not only can you, but I like to."

Pierre took her back to the house and watched her drive away and then he went in.

The Hunter house was tall and creaky, with dusty green vases on wooden tables and narrow stairways that climbed high into the shadows, and Pierre's parents were in the living room watching the movie *She Wore a Yellow Ribbon*.

Monster, the black Lab, slept in flat profile on the faded red carpet.

Pierre felt his way into a black leather chair while watching the TV screen, and he considered telling them what Carrie Sloan had said, but then he thought that probably he wouldn't.

"Why is this a classic?" said his mother. "I really want to know. It's all about singing and transportation as far as I can tell."

Pierre's father picked up the newspaper and rattled it and put on his glasses and read. "It has 'an elegiac quality of the Western vastness.'"

"That doesn't even make sense."

"'Among John Wayne's finest performances.'"

"Maybe. But when I see him I don't see anything but John Wayne."

"That's what a star is."

"I think it's better when the hero is sort of unassuming and you don't know who it will be."

Pierre put his legs up and watched the TV over his knees. "Tell me again why she wears the yellow ribbon."

"She wears it for her lover in the U.S. Cavalry."

"Look, Monster," said Pierre's father. "There's a dog in John Wayne's regiment."

He talked to Monster all the time and often replied for her in a voice higher and denser than his own.

"What about a walk, girl?" he would say, holding the leash in his hands and looking down at the Lab's deep and skeptical eyes.

"I don't know. Looks pretty rainy."

"Oh, you'll love it. Come on."

"Pretty fucking rainy out there."

"I thought you were supposed to be a water dog."

"Yeah, you know, that's really overstated. I'm going to go lie down now."

"No, let me put your leash on."

"Go ahead, you won't like it."

"On you, I mean...."

Pierre's parents were eccentric and admired figures in Shale. They had arrived in town in the middle of their lives, having divorced other spouses and left other families in far-off Council Bluffs.

The scandal of this was apparent but never seemed to touch them somehow. They worked hard, paid attention to the world, and threw raucous card parties. They had Pierre at an age when many parents, themselves included, had children who were almost grown.

Pierre's mother managed the insurance office in Shale and his father was an electrophysicist for an aerospace fabricator in Desmond City. No one understood what that amounted to, not even Pierre. His father could explain it, but only in the sort of language that the human mind tends to forget in an instant.

Once, when Pierre was fourteen, he and the Labrador pup Monster were nosing around in the basement and found a pair of ice skates hanging by frayed laces on a nail in the basement. The skates were well made and heavy but scuffed and scarred and brittle with age. He took them down and carried them upstairs.

He found his father in his study, where he was on the telephone with someone at the lab where he worked.

"Try shaking it," he said. "You did, huh? Well, redo it then. . . . I don't care. Just lay it on the table for the time being. . . . Don't worry about that. It just doesn't. That's what everybody says. . . . Where does the capacitance come from? See what I mean. It's got to come from somewhere."

He looked at Pierre. "I'm on hold," he said.

"Are these yours?" said Pierre.

"I'm surprised they're still around. I used to play hockey, you know. Wasn't too bad at it, either."

"Can I have them?" said Pierre.

His father nodded. "Sure, take them."

Into the phone he said, "Yeah. . . . No, no, no. Did you read chapter eight? I'm pretty sure it's in there. . . . Well, read it again."

Pierre tried to work up a stormy heart of romantic loss about breaking up with Rebecca. It gave him license to drink and brood with hard eyes, which he found interesting.

After he got hammered one night at a high place above Lens Lake called the Grade, his parents found him standing in the kitchen.

"What if there was a language with only one word in it?" he asked.

"It would be easy to learn," said his mother.

"And with that word they would say everything, every time they spoke," said Pierre.

"Yeah, that would be some language," said his father. "What are you on?"

"Just drinking," said Pierre. "Just good old American drinking. You seem old tonight. You both seem old."

This was honest, though a crummy thing to say, and he would have reason to regret it.

"You make us old," said his mother. "The way you go around, Pierre, I wonder what will become of you."

"You're not even sad," said his father. "Not really. You're just trying to steal the spotlight of Rebecca's illness."

"It's possible but not probable," said Pierre.

His father drew a glass of water from the faucet and gave it to him. "Drink this," he said. "Maybe you should have gone to boarding school. I don't know if it's been so good for you around here."

"I wouldn't mind if they had lacrosse," said Pierre. "And I think most of them do."

"You play football."

"I like those lacrosse sticks, though."

"This came for you," said his mother.

It was a letter from Rebecca, which Pierre took up to his room to read in bed.

Dear Pierre,

I can't believe senior year beckons and with it our last chance to do the things that will last a lifetime in our memories. Whoever said every day is a gift from

somewhere really had the right outlook. As Carrie told
you, I want to be free to see other people in our last year
at Shale-Midlothian High. Always remember how I
wore your coat on the field trip to Effigy Mounds.

Yours truly,
Rebecca

Pierre let the letter sail down to the floor. It sounded as if she were dating a class-ring salesman, though he was touched that she remembered wearing his coat. But they never did get back together, and the following year Rebecca moved to Arizona, where her father took a job with the city of Yuma, and Pierre never saw her again.

The years went by. Pierre went off to college in Ames, 175 miles south and west. It took him five years to finish. His parents died the winter of his third year. His mother's death had been predicted for some time, but his father's heart quit on him without warning three weeks later. His father was coming home from the hardware store in Shale and pulled over to the side of the road, where a mailwoman making her rounds found him in his car.

When Pierre looked back on that time it was as if he were seeing it through clouded glass. He moved like a sleepwalker among people in suits and dresses, people hovering in stairwells. That his parents were gone seemed impossible. He thought of them as still alive. The problem loomed but the solution was out of reach. It felt like there was still something he might do if only he could think of it.

A kind of nervous seizure came upon him as he waited for his father's funeral to begin at the Church of the Four Corners. His hands shook and his breath grew short. He got up and sidled down the row of half-siblings from Council Bluffs. He left the main part of the church and went up two stories to the bell tower and stood looking out over the half wall at the sunlight on the snow-covered hills. He smoked a cigarette and put it out and then he cried pretty hard and for a long while. He had a blue handkerchief like the old farmers carried, and with it he wiped his face and blew his nose. The light bothered his eyes because it was so bright and thin and evidently unaware of what it was shining on.

TWO

THE STRANGE chain of events that would end in the famous violence on Fay's Hill began on New Year's Eve of the year that Pierre turned twenty-four.

He was living in Shale again, in an apartment above the stationery store. He had a bachelor's degree in science and a job as a bartender at a supper club called the Jack of Diamonds out by Lens Lake.

He was the youngest bartender by a number of years and so he was given the early shift that night, before the customers would be laying down the big careless tips of the end of the year.

Thus Pierre left the bar around nine o'clock and went to a house party in Desmond City. The house belonged to some people he didn't know very well and was arranged in a stark and random style. There was a hammer in the bathtub, a Bakelite radio in the fireplace, and guitars and drums in the living room. Torn paper blinds lay over the back of a bench near the windows, as if someone had taken them down but forgot to throw them away. The walls were painted dark red and blue.

Appropriated advertising art was not unusual in such a house and the example they had found was rare and hypnotic. It was a clear blue brick in the shape of a pack of cigarettes but three or four times larger, and the inside was alive with perpetual lightning. Touching the surface brought a swarm of rays to your fingertips. The surgeon general's warning was printed on the side of the display, and on the front it said:

Kool
Milds
The House of Menthol

Pierre got a tumbler of whiskey from the kitchen and sat in a rocking chair drinking and watching the blue light. After a while a woman came and sat on the arm of the chair. She was rangy and mascaraed and she smelled like spice and wore a black leather jacket with silver studs and thick fringe down the sleeves.

Her name was Allison Kennedy, and she worked on the line at the glass factory in the town of Arcadia. She had ice-colored eyes with gold flecks and sang in a band called the Carbon Family.

"Somebody said you play drums," she said.

"Yeah," he said. "That and cello."

"We're trying to get something going, but our drummer's not here."

"I'll play."

The music started in half an hour or so. Allison Kennedy had a red ASAT Classic and there were two other guitarists and Pierre on the drums. The little amps sat back by the wall, throwing out a big jangling sound. They played "Thrift Store Chair," "Coralville Dam," "Polyester Bride," and "In Heaven There Is No Beer."

Few played the last song as the Carbon Family did. It was a slow version full of minor chords and sorrow. With her highest ghostly voice, Allison Kennedy made you believe it was true.

> *In Heaven there is no ale*
> *And no one delivers the mail*
> *And when our heartbeats fail*
> *Our friends will attend the rummage sale*

The song ended, but the despair of it remained in the heat of the party room. The band members walked off to have a beer and figure out what to play next. Pierre stayed at the drums. There was a bass with two mounted toms, a snare, a floor tom, and two cymbals, a ride and a high-hat. He began a solo that roamed around, gathering volume and speed and always coming back to a series of rim shots that sounded like a machine breaking down.

Yes, we will die—this was the message of his drumming —but until then we must make a big racket like this one. He was trying to restore the psychic balance of the party, but once people know a drum solo is under way they will usually leave the room no matter why the solo is being played, or at least that's what happened in this case.

The band's drummer arrived. Pierre walked around the party with his tall glass of whiskey, listening to conversations and sometimes joining in, but he never seemed to say the right thing. It's funny how you can become the unwelcome guest when you don't know that many people, and should be at worst simply a stranger, but Pierre had a knack for it.

Once, for example, he found a boy and two girls talking in an alcove between the kitchen and some other room. They had the bright quick eyes and Goodwill wardrobe of students from the junior college.

"They told me I was supposed to take them," said the boy. "And I did. But my ears started ringing worse than ever so I stopped."

"Taking what?" Pierre asked.

"Was I talking to you?"

"Not till now."

"Antidepressants."

"Are you sad?"

"I'm depressed."

Pierre nodded and took a drink. "What's the difference?"

"This is just what I'm talking about," said the boy.

One of the girls looked flatly at Pierre and chewed on a small plastic sword. "It's a common misunderstanding about depression that it has to do with something depressing," she said.

"You should try listening to music," said Pierre. "It always makes me feel better."

"I'm sure it's that simple," said the boy.

"The Decemberists have a good album out. Listen to 'The Sporting Life.' If that doesn't make you smile, nothing will."

"Who are you?"

"He's the one that was smashing on the drums," said the girl.

"Oh," said Pierre. "Did you like that?"

"Not really. It hurt my ears."

So Pierre was not doing that well at the party but could not seem to help himself. And yet sometimes, just when you least deserve it, something good happens.

Pierre was coming down the stairs and Allison Kennedy in the black fringed jacket was going up and they saw each other in the narrow stairwell and without a word began making out.

This was the kind of thing that never happened to Pierre, and he felt that the desperate kisses were absolving him of the drum solo and of bothering the depressed student.

Then it was over—he went down and Allison went up—but he understood that some part of the night might be salvaged, and he found his gloves and coat and went outside to take a walk and sober up a little if he could.

He walked to a park down the street where he could look up and see if anything changed when the year gave way to another one—as if the starpaper sky might fade out and reappear in a different pattern.

Pierre wore a herringbone overcoat of black and gray, and yellow leather gloves with straps across the back, and once he was outside of the dark-walled house he congratulated himself on moving with great coordination down the sidewalk and into the park.

There was nothing unusual going on in the sky. He did see a falling star, but they were so common on winter nights in that place that it would have been more out of the ordinary not to see one if you looked up for any time at all.

In the picnic shelter of the park an old man was sitting on a table with his hands in his coat pockets and black cowboy boots resting on the bench, and Pierre walked over to talk to him.

"Happy New Year," said Pierre.

"And to you."

"What are you doing?"

"Waiting for somebody. Almost beginning to think they made other plans."

Pierre tried to put his foot up on the cement floor of the picnic shelter but he missed, so he tried again and made it.

"Been drinking?" said the old man.

"A little bit."

"Well, this is the night for it, I guess."

"I'm at a party up the street."

"Are you ready?"

"For what?"

"I don't know. The new year. Whatever it brings."

"More than ready."

"Good. Let's shake on it."

They took off their gloves and shook hands.

"Listen," said Pierre. "It's pretty cold out here. Why don't you come along to this party I was telling you about."

"Oh, I don't think so. Painful introductions. Onion dip on the table. It's not for me."

"It's just a circus anyway. Nobody knows who's in one room from the next."

"You go alone. I'm sure you'll find it."

When Pierre was out of sight, the old man got up and walked across the park to the street where his car was parked. His name was Tim Geer. He drove north out of Desmond City and up through Shale to a house on the bluff above the lake. He got out of the car and knocked on the door, where he was met by a young woman in faded jeans, red socks, and a black felt shirt. She invited him in and poured two glasses of champagne, and they sat in the house and talked.

"He made it," said Tim. "Showed up at midnight."

"How do you know it's him?" she said.

"He wouldn't have been there otherwise. And you've seen the skater, right?"

"Yeah."

"Well, he's the skater."

"When does that happen?"

"Not for a while. You'll know."

"It seems kind of underhanded, doesn't it?"

"Can't be helped, Stella. You came here out of a pretty bad situation, if you remember."

"Yes."

"And the one that put you there has got to be found. That's only right. And you can't do it, and I can't do it."

"But this guy can."

"I think so."

"How?"

"I don't know. That's for him to figure out."

Pierre walked back to the party. Everything looked different following his encounter with the old man—the cars along the road seemed newer, the snow less trampled upon. And when he opened the door and walked into the house, he realized that he was at the wrong party.

Momentum or perhaps fear of embarrassment carried him across the living room, and he sat down in an easy chair. The two parties were very different. Here the floors were polished hardwood with a vibrant green rug in the center, and there were flower paintings on the walls, and middle-aged people had gathered around a piano by the picture window to sing "This Magic Moment." They had lyric sheets and dark pewter mugs to swing back and forth, keeping time like happy people on a television show.

The music stopped after a while. The piano faltered and the voices died away. A man in an embroidered vest led the group from the piano to the chair where Pierre was sitting. The man was short and burly and the vest illustrated an alpine scene in which a horse cart had overturned, spilling riders into the snow, and the horses stood looking back over their shoulders. There was a little story going on right in that vest.

"Do you know someone here?" said the man.

"I don't think so."

"Then what might I ask are you doing?"

"I was at a party," said Pierre. "But it wasn't this party. I don't really understand what's going on."

"Someone's private home is what's going on. And you have to leave. I'm an off-duty police officer."

"I'm a bartender."

"Tell you what we're going to do, and that is, Get up and walk out of here like none of this ever happened."

"Is there onion dip on the table?" said Pierre.

"Onion."

"Yeah."

"Never mind what's on the table."

"Do you want to see my coin trick?"

"No."

But then a woman spoke up on Pierre's behalf.

"Oh for God's sakes let him do his coin trick," she said. "The poor kid only wants to do a coin trick on New Year's Eve."

She had curly blond hair and her face was flushed and she wore a straw hat with a broken brim.

"He's drunk," said the cop. "I guess you would know all about that."

"Oh, let him do his coin trick," she said.

People gave her the cold eye for having broken their unity against the intruding Pierre, but it also seemed that she had taken the upper hand of the argument by bringing the spirit of the New Year into it. It was like patriotism in that you could throw it out there on the side of whatever ill-advised thing you wanted to do. And let's face it, most people will take the time to watch a good coin trick, or any coin trick, and they can decide later whether it is good or not.

Pierre got up and took off his gloves and coat and tossed them on the chair. The cop in the mountain vest turned his back and raised his hands as if to put an end to his role in whatever happened next.

"Ladies and gentlemen, I would ask you now for your spare change," said Pierre.

They came up with quite a lot, probably five dollars' worth, including seven dimes, which would complicate the trick but make it more impressive if it worked. Or impressive might be overstating it, because it was a pretty common trick, and really wasn't a trick at all.

Pierre stacked the coins carefully. That was critical. Quarters on the bottom, then nickels, then pennies, then dimes. He secured the stack between the thumb and first two fingers of his left hand. Then he cocked his right arm up and beside his head as if he were going to throw a baseball using only the motion of the forearm. With his left hand he set the stack of coins out on the flat of his raised right elbow. When he was satisfied that the coins would not fall he withdrew his left hand, letting it fall to his side, and looked at the partygoers. They looked at the coins, which formed a trembling tower out at the end of the lonely pier of his inverted forearm. Then he moved his right arm forward with such speed that the open hand caught the coins with a steely snap just as the elbow dropped away from them.

Not one coin flew wild or fell to the floor. Not one stuck out between Pierre's closed fingers. The people loved it. They clapped and whistled and forgot for a moment that Pierre was only a stranger who had wandered into the house. It was a small bit of perfection, so rare in this fractured world. And he held out his hand and opened it to reveal the fistful of coins.

"Okay, trick's over, very nice, shove off," said the off-duty policeman.

Pierre left the party he had not been meant to attend and stood looking up and down the street wondering where in hell the other party was.

As he did so, a police cruiser pulled up in the street with its blue lights wheeling on the snow.

The police officers talked over what to do. Though Pierre was out of the house to which they'd been summoned, there was no telling he wouldn't go into some other house. And they had come all this way.

So it was not a hard decision. They put him in the back of the cruiser and took him to the jail. He argued a little but didn't care that much as he was still caught up in the success of the coin trick.

"Swing by the park," he said. "There's this old guy there and I want to make sure he didn't freeze."

"You ought to worry about yourself," said one of the officers.

At the jail they fingerprinted him and took the things from his pockets and put him in a cell. Thick chains anchored a plank to the wall for a bed and a shaft of light came through a window. It was cold and there was ink all over his hands.

Pierre remembered the movie *Modern Times* and the cell that Charlie Chaplin did not want to leave. This was not that absurdly homey place but it was not so bad. He lay down on the bunk and thought about kissing Allison Kennedy on the stairs at the first party.

He always had to have something to think about when he went to sleep. That way if he woke up in the middle of the night the thing that he had been thinking about would be waiting for him to take up again and his mind wouldn't race in all directions.

She had been warm and unexpected with her scented hair and fool's-gold eyes. And reliving that moment on the stairs, Pierre passed the night away in the Desmond City jail.

THREE

PIERRE'S LAWYER called one Sunday afternoon in February when Pierre was in his apartment in Shale with all his stuff around him: cello, books, and model boats. A wooden box on top of the TV held the ashes of the dog Monster.

He hadn't played the cello much since high school and the calluses were gone from his fingers, but still he brought it out from the corner sometimes and played the theme from the movie *Martian Summer*, which was a good song and slow enough that he could still make it sound all right.

The lawyer was calling from the clubhouse of the golf course, where he was in a card game with the prosecutor, and the lawyer and the prosecutor had made a deal on Pierre's case, which was to be heard on Tuesday.

"How are the cards going?" Pierre said.

"I'm behind. But that's how I play."

"Are they dropping the charges?"

"They are and they aren't. Come on up, I'll tell you all about it."

Pierre put on his boots and laced them up and picked up his father's old ice skates in the kitchen. He took them down the back stairs to the alley and slung them into the trunk of his car.

The road lay black and narrow with a coat of ice you might not know about until you hit the brakes—at which point you'd find out fast—and the wind carried a grit that was part snow and part dirt and swept the windshield with a dry metallic sound.

Shale was on a plateau in the Driftless Area and the ridges ran north from it, dense with forest and moving apart like the splayed fingers of a hand. It used to be said that the glaciers steered around the Driftless Area entirely, but as Pierre understood the modern geological point of view, this was not accurate, though he liked to think it was—to picture the glaciers lifting their blue foreheads, taking their bearings, and splitting up with an agreement to meet down the line.

The road ran out along the ridge and gradually veered off and down into the shadows of the state forest that rose in banks on either side. In a few miles Pierre passed the Jack of Diamonds, where he would be working later that day, and, a little farther, on a movie house called the Small Art Cinema. They were the only businesses between Shale and Lens Lake, and each occupied a fringe of gravel carved out of the part of the forest known as Fay's Hill.

Pierre went up along the lake and west on the Eden Center Road. The sky was cloudy, the highway empty, and lights shone in house windows, though it was only midafternoon, creating an excellent sense of isolation that made most any destination seem profound and mysterious.

This was true even if you were going to the Lens Lake Country Club. It gave off a sadness that was a residue of the wasted summers beneath the snow. White hills rolled into nothing and the ball-washing stations stood here and there like random red sentries in a cold country.

Carrie Sloan—or Carrie Miles, as she was married now, to Pierre's friend Roland Miles—worked in the clubhouse and had written a poem about the course in winter. She did not think much of the poem, but Pierre had read it and he remembered it now:

> *Pain is in the water,*
> *Despair is in the rough,*
> *Envy takes a mulligan*
> *And Death has seen enough.*
> *She's coming to the clubhouse*
> *To have a drink with you.*
> *Her foursome takes forever;*
> *She's on the green in two.*

Carrie had written a number of poems about the golf course, and they leaned toward the fatalistic or existential. It was not that her life was so tragic but that she found gloom more interesting than the everyday world.

Pierre walked into the clubhouse and saw the five men playing cards at a table near the fireplace. They weren't talking but only picking up cards and looking at them and putting them down. He wasn't about to stroll up to the table, as he felt that any little word could mess up the flow of the game. And so he stood watching until his lawyer saw him and got up.

They talked beneath the large aerial photo of Shale on the wall. It was forty years old and the funny thing was that there had been an accident on Main Street just before it was taken, although you wouldn't know this unless someone explained it to you.

That is, you could see the cars and the people standing in the street, but it didn't look like anything out of the ordinary. So, really, it wasn't that funny, it was just called funny.

"This will be over on Tuesday, right?" said Pierre.

The lawyer was a small man in his middle thirties with a serene smile and enormous eyeglasses, covering a great expanse of his face.

"That depends on you," said the lawyer. "Were you in my office Friday?"

"Yeah, I read all the magazines."

"I thought so. Sorry about that. I got tied up with some ungodly quitclaim and the people are dead and nobody knows anything. But here's the deal. The prosecutor and I were kicking something around, and I wanted to know what you think before we kick it any further."

"Okay."

"They drop the trespassing. I know you'll want to hear that because we've talked about it. They don't have it. They know they don't have it. Forget it. It's gone."

"Which one is the prosecutor?"

"He's the one over there. He's looking at his watch. Now he's hitting it, like maybe it isn't working right."

"Should I meet him, since I'm here?"

"I wouldn't. He's way down."

"How are you?"

"Almost back to nothing."

"Well, they shouldn't make the charge if they don't have it."

"Of course, we would say that, but they're not us," said the lawyer. "It's how they do things, and that way they have something to trade. Is it right? In a perfect world, I don't guess it is. But try finding that world."

"And in exchange, I do what?"

"Plead out to the public intoxication."

"Guilty."

"As charged."

"I thought I'd get out of this."

"You are. I'm coming to that. Because what you do is turn around and apply for Accelerated Rehabilitation, and they won't contest it. So no conviction is ever written down; there is no conviction, if you complete the prescribed thing. Which is half a dozen classes on alcohol and so forth."

"This is my best option."

"And a good one, I think."

"I was intoxicated."

"Sure you were. Why else would you barge in somebody's house you don't even know?"

"But it wasn't trespassing."

"I just said that."

"Because they asked me, in the house. When I said I would do a trick, they said, 'Fine. Do it.'"

"And dress up a little bit for court. That's the other thing. Dress like your father did. That was a man who was a sharp dresser and a hell of a guy."

"Yeah."

"You know, I felt bad when they died. But then I thought about it, after while, and I thought maybe that's what you would want. To go together, I mean."

"A lot of people said that," said Pierre. "And I don't know that it isn't true."

They looked down. Chair legs scraped on the tiles and the prosecutor crossed the room, cracking his knuckles.

"Tell me something I don't understand," he said. "What motivates someone to call a twenty-dollar bet when here I sit with three kings and get knocked off by some illegitimate fucking straight?"

"I don't know," said Pierre's lawyer. "The way some people play, it defies logic."

"I mean, kings? Come on. You can't *not* play them."

"No, I agree with that. You've got to play kings. Say, this is Pierre Hunter."

"Oh, sure. The trespasser. Are you with us here, so we can all get on with our lives?"

"Yeah. It's fair."

"Kings," said the prosecutor, unable to get over how he had lost the hand.

Pierre left the clubhouse, opened the trunk of his car, and took out the ice skates. He walked down to the frozen creek and sat on the footbridge to put the skates on. Then he tied the laces of his boots together and slung them over his shoulder.

He set off down the creek, skating east. He would wear the good clothes and be humble in court. The evidence called for humility. Yet he was not troubled. When he did foolish things he had a way of putting them behind him, as if he did not know the person who had done them. And it was just as well, he thought, for they could not be called back.

The creek meandered across the golf course, through a field of brush and low hills, and down to the northern shore of Lens Lake. Pierre got on the lake and headed south. The lake was long and ringed with gray hills and yellow bluffs, and it made for a fast skate what with the wind at his back and the long silver plane of the ice. He was no great skater, but traveling in a straight line in this way he felt strong and athletic.

Going back of course was another story, but he did not have to go back, because the Jack of Diamonds was not far from the southern end of the lake, and he could walk from the lake to the tavern, as he had many times, and catch a ride back to his car at the end of the night.

In the middle of the lake a crosscurrent moved in from the west and little twisters of old dry snow rose and fell and the wind riffled the swelled and foxed pages of a magazine lying on the ice. *Popular Mechanics,* Pierre saw as he went by. It seemed odd. He turned a wide circle back to see what was on the cover. It was a story about the U.S. government's top-secret plan for dealing with UFOs should they arrive.

As it happened, Pierre had seen a UFO when he was young. It was a classic sort of flying saucer with lights around the perimeter, and it buzzed the Hunter house and seemed to sink behind a row of grain bins down the road. No one believed him. Why would they? The next day he went looking for traces of the landing without luck. But he'd had an interest in aliens ever since and did not want to know what the U.S. government had in store for them.

So he skated on, digging in with the blades and raising his arms to increase the sail capacity of his coat.

Pierre hit bad ice at the southern end of the lake. It came up on him, or he came up on it, without warning. Sometimes because of the light there are shadings that you can't see until you are almost on top of them. And he never worried too much about the thickness of the ice because it had always been thick enough. He had skated over dark ice many times without a trace of give.

This time, though, he tried to turn back, because he saw that the field into which he had gone was deep and ominous, surrounding him on three sides. But he was moving too fast. The quick stop with shaved flying ice was a maneuver beyond his skill level. He did get turned around but not by much and the wind carried him backward into the thin ice. There was no groaning or cracking, none of the slow collapse you would expect. Instead the ice gave way at once and Pierre disappeared into the water.

The light went out and he felt the cold before he understood what had happened, obvious as it was. It felt more like fire than ice, as if his skin were cracking into pieces. He had nothing to stand on. His own boots were floating up from his shoulder and bumping him in the face.

Kicking and thrashing he made the surface after a time and swam to the ice that last held him up and he laid his arms out on it. It seemed solid enough. He hung there breathing hard and looking around. It was a quiet day on the lake. Fishing houses stood far off like archaeology. Somewhere beyond the bluffs a snowmobile droned in fitful progress.

His face was cold in the wind. With a soaked sleeve he scraped water from it. Not much help in that. It seemed that if he could push up on his arms he might simply fall forward onto the ice. So he tried that, but as he moved up and put weight on his elbows the ice broke again and he was back in the water. Three times he did this and three times fought back to the receding shelf of ice. Then he tried bringing a leg up, thinking maybe he could get a blade to catch. But the landing of his foot broke the ice again, only now it was a longer piece that broke. All he was doing was making an ever-widening channel of open water.

After twenty minutes he was too cold and tired to go on heaving himself up and breaking the ice. He thought of calling for help but this seemed so close to defeat that he wouldn't do it. He wouldn't make a sound. He rested on the ice and watched the light going out of the sky.

Pierre heard someone asking if he was all right. He looked up. A woman in a long orange coat and fur-lined hood stood some distance off on the ice. She had a coil of rope, a mallet, and a stake.

"Hang on," she said.

She dropped the rope, fell to her knees, and hammered the stake into the ice so that it angled away from Pierre. She took the stake in both hands to test the hold and then wrapped the end of the yellow and orange rope around it three times and tied it off in a double knot.

She got up and walked toward him, playing the rope out along the ice.

"Don't come any closer," said Pierre.

"I won't."

Some twenty-five feet away she stopped and threw the remaining coil toward him. It took several tries before the rope fell within reach of his hands.

"Just get a good hold on it," she said.

Pierre gathered the line and closed his hands around it. The woman in the orange coat went back and took up the slack and wound it around the stake. Then she set herself sideways behind the stake, planting her left foot against it, and began pulling in the rope. And in this way Pierre at last reached ice that would hold him and he slid onto it and turned onto his back and lay there looking at the sky.

"Don't get up," said the woman. "Just roll away from the water. You want to keep your weight spread out."

Pierre did so. His boots, which were still tied over his shoulder, got in the way and he freed them and slid them away from him. Cold and exhausted, he nonetheless felt self-conscious to be slowly rolling across the lake. Then he got up, retrieved the boots, and walked to her on the blades of his skates.

"Thank you," he said.

"I was up on the hill and I saw you skating," she said. "Then there were some trees in the way, and I could see where you would come out, but you never did."

She began coiling the rope and Pierre looked at the stake, which was a length of rebar with a red epoxy coating.

"Have you done this before?" he said.

"No. But I've thought about how I would."

Then she put the rope over her shoulder and took the mallet and knocked the stake through the ice and into the water.

"Come on," she said.

They made their way to the shore, giving wide berth to the wandering slick of watery ice. She said her name was Stella Rosmarin and she lived in a house on the bluff. They crossed the narrow beach and came to stone steps that rose east to west across the rock wall. Pierre sat down to remove the drenched skates and replace them with the boots that were in the same condition. He told her his name. Then they went up.

It was a yellow two-story house in a clearing set back a hundred yards from the edge of the land. Sashes of frost were in the windows and evergreen trees stood all around with their dark branches separated by the weight of snow.

They went into the house where it was warm and Stella put her hood back and took her coat off and hung it on the back of a chair in the kitchen. Pierre had imagined that she would be beautiful—reflexively, as he did when hearing women's voices on the radio—but he was not prepared for how beautiful she was.

Slender, in a white thermal shirt and deep green corduroys. Curved hips, narrow waist. Brilliant shoulders, delicate yet purposeful, like wings. Strong arms—as he knew. Long and graceful neck. Thick dark hair down her back. Full, serious mouth. Dark eyes. Some hurt or concern in the eyes that he could not trace.

He stood looking at her with the water from his wool coat dripping around his feet.

"You need to get out of those things," she said.

"I can change over to the bar," he said. "But I would take a ride there if you could."

"I don't have a car," she said.

"Do you have a clothes dryer?"

She showed him the back room where the washer and dryer were. He closed the door and got undressed and put his coat and clothes in the dryer. A big green towel was in a wicker basket and he dried off with it.

Then she handed a white bathrobe around the door and he put it on and tied the cord and put the green towel around his neck like a millionaire taking it easy at the health club.

The robe was thick and soft and smelled like the inside of an orange peel. It occurred to him that she had worn it, and now he was wearing it, and so it was like touching her, once removed.

They drank tea and whiskey at the kitchen table as his clothes rolled around in the dryer and his boots steamed in the oven.

"I think I saved your life, Pierre," she said.

"I think you did too."

"You should never skate alone."

On the table was a bonsai tree in a terra-cotta tray with pebbles and moss and tiny branches that bent to the side as if blown by the wind.

"And now I owe you a great favor," said Pierre, "that only I can do."

"Is that how it works?"

"Doesn't it? In stories, anyway."

"And what would that be?"

"You wouldn't know till the time comes," said Pierre. "A messenger arrives: *Your horse is waiting*. You know. *The hour is upon us*."

"Do you ride horses?"

"No. But you'd be able to all of a sudden. You'd find that you could. Or not, and you would fall off."

"Maybe you have hypothermia," she said.

"What are the symptoms?"

"Confusion, I know."

"Actually I feel pretty good."

"So do I."

"Do you live here all the time?" he said.

"Yes."

"It seems quiet."

"This place was left to me," she said. "I came from Wisconsin, it was last summer. I needed somewhere to stay, and there was no one here, so it seemed to make sense."

"Why did you need somewhere to stay?"

"Oh, it's a long story. Maybe I'll tell you someday."

"How do you get around without a car?"

"I don't, very much," she said. "I have a bicycle."

"Not much good this time of year."

"No, that's true. They deliver my groceries, and the

mailman comes, and the meterman, though he doesn't come that often, compared to the mailman."

"It sounds kind of lonely."

"It is, but I haven't minded so much. I guess you could say I've been waiting."

"For what?"

She bent her head to blow steam from the tea as she held the cup in both hands.

"I don't know," she said. "You, maybe. To pull you out of the lake."

The dryer completed its cycle, and Pierre got dressed, said goodbye to Stella, and left the house. Her driveway wound down through the trees to the Lake Road, where he turned south and headed for the Jack of Diamonds. It was dark. His clothes were dry, and though his boots had seemed dry enough in the kitchen of Stella's house, they were wet and cold now, and he stamped his feet on the pavement to keep them warm.

I'll have to go back and see her again, he thought.

FOUR

THE JACK of Diamonds was a low building of dark dovetailed timbers and square yellow windows set against the bank of the forest. Pierre went around to the side, through the kitchen, and down to the basement, where he had a locker with dry socks and sneakers. He put them on and went upstairs.

Chris Garner and Larry Rudd were sitting at the bar. They came in three or four times a week to drink beer and talk of obscure subjects and everyday items, such as rotary weed trimmers or garbage disposals, that were more dangerous than commonly understood. They were in their fifties and had been teammates on a basketball team that almost went to the state tournament many years ago. Now Rudd owned two vacuum-cleaner stores and Garner sold shoes.

Pierre rearranged the liquor bottles as they talked. He grouped them by color, which other bartenders found unprofessional, because blue gins would end up next to blue vodkas, for example, but so be it.

"Oh, we watched it," said Rudd. "The wife and me, in the comfort of our home. Watched the whole movie. But if that's supposed to be sexy, I don't know, I must be missing something."

"Because of the masks," said Garner.

"Yeah. You couldn't tell who anybody was."

"But that's the idea, though, isn't it. The anonymity. That it would tend to make it more exciting."

"Not knowing what somebody looks like?" said Rudd. "What's exciting about that?"

"Well, it depends on the mask, I guess. If it was like the Lone Ranger wore, you would have a pretty good idea of the overall appearance."

"Nah, these were over their whole faces. They were supposed to be—I don't know what. Cats. Spirits of the past. Birds. I believe there were birds. Lords and ladies."

"Frightening things," suggested Garner. "At, like, a ball or something."

"Well, again, that may have been the intention. But to me it was very implausible."

"Maybe it's different for young people," said Garner. "Pierre, get in on this."

"What's the question?" said Pierre.

"Would you sleep with some woman if you didn't know who it was because she was wearing a mask?"

"That's what you're asking."

"Rudd seen a movie about that."

"I don't know."

"But you might."

"It's possible."

"Pierre, you dog."

"You guys about ready?"

Pierre drew two beers, poured off the foam, topped the glasses up, and set them on the bar.

"A face is kind of a mask anyway, when you think about it," he said.

Rudd took a drink and set the glass down. "You should never ask Pierre anything."

"You don't make your face," said Pierre. "It's given to you. You might think it represents your true self, but why would it? Half the time you make an expression and think, Oh, this is my whatever expression, and nobody even knows what you're thinking."

"That's true," said Garner. "I have no idea what my face looks like to the outside world."

"That's just as well," said Rudd. "So anyway, we get done watching this sex movie with all the masks, and I go out to the kitchen, and there's some water standing in the sink. So what do I do? I run the garbage disposal, right, as that's the only way to get rid of the water. And this is my problem with them: that you can't just pull some simple plug but you have to fire up the equivalent of an outboard motor to get the fucking water out of the sink—when what should come shooting out but this huge shard of blue glass. I was lucky it didn't kill me."

Pierre gave last call at the end of the night, and everyone but Chris Garner went home. The shoe salesman lived alone and was often the last to leave. He sat at a table near the bar with a Rusty Nail he'd been working on for some time. Pierre carted kegs up to the walk-in cooler and then went behind the bar, where he stood counting money and putting it in the cash box.

"Do you believe in fate, Chris?" he said.

"Fate."

"Yeah. That things happen for a reason."

"Sometimes. Like if your car won't start, and you left the lights on, that's probably why."

"That's not fate."

"I didn't say it was."

"Fate is more like you leaving your lights on in order that the car won't start."

"Who would do that?"

"Nobody, on purpose. But if you were meant to."

"Then no. I would have to say I don't believe it. You must, however, or you wouldn't raise the question."

"I'm not sure."

"You should ask Rudd. He would know."

"Yeah?"

"Or if he didn't, he would make something up."

Terry Benton, owner of the Jack of Diamonds, came in at half past midnight. His story was one of those you read about from time to time. He had made a lot of money designing computer networks in Oregon and retired nine years ago at the age of forty-four to return to the Midwest and start a supper club. His idea had been to re-create an earlier Jack of Diamonds, which had been in Eden Center and which he remembered from his childhood.

"Any trouble tonight?" he said.

"Nope," said Pierre.

"How'd we do?"

"Better than last Sunday."

"Last Sunday wasn't bad."

"Yeah, so ... better than that."

Terry laid his camel-hair coat along the bar, sat down, and turned toward the room. He had a deceptive build—wide of frame but not very deep, as if he had been flattened by a cartoon steamroller. "Do you like the chairs?"

"I guess so," said Pierre. "What about them?"

"I don't know. I'm not sure about the red vinyl anymore."

"What would you get, wood?"

"I'm thinking about it."

"Can't hardly go wrong with wood," said Pierre.

"The red might be too busy."

"I fell in the lake today."

"Did you?"

"I was skating."

"You wouldn't catch me on that lake."

"Why?"

"Why? Because you fall in. What's wrong with Garner?"

Pierre shrugged and raised his eyebrows.

Terry walked out among the tables, swinging his arms and clapping his hands. "Let's be going home, Chris."

"All right, all right," said Garner. He stood and put on his overcoat. He adjusted the lapels and shook his head and walked with Terry to the door.

"You could use some new shoes," he said. "Why don't you stop in one of these times?"

"Maybe I will. But tell me something. What's your opinion of the chairs?"

"They seem fine to me, Terry."

Terry had a lot invested in the place. He'd outfitted the kitchen with Ramhold-Bailer appliances, hired the chef Keith Lyon away from the Chanticleer in Austin, Minnesota, and commissioned an artist to paint murals on the walls. In the style of Grant Wood, the murals portrayed the surrounding countryside as a nearsighted dream in which everything was smoother and greener and more discrete than in life. The bar itself was cherrywood and stable as stone.

Terry had wanted the restaurant to be suave, for that is how he remembered the original, but he also wanted it to be popular, and he seemed flexible as to how this might be achieved.

You could see this in his reaction to the incident of the sink and the sign. Late one night about a year before, a man who had been shut off from drinking anymore went into the men's room and tore the sink off the wall. He was banned for life but that was not the end of it. A couple of days later a homemade sign appeared in the ditch along the Lake Road leading to the Jack of Diamonds. It was black paint on white plywood, and what it said was:

TWO MILES TO THE
STINKING GREASE PIT

Well, there was no question who had put up the sign. It was obviously the man who had wrecked the sink and flooded the men's room. And at their weekly meeting most of the employees agreed that the thing to do was to pull up the sign and throw it away.

But Terry said, "Let's think about this."

He said, "We are not afraid of this accusation. It's laughable. The Jack happens to have Keith Lyon, probably the best chef in the Driftless Area."

Terry was always trying to get people to call the Jack of Diamonds "the Jack," as he thought it sounded hipper and more inviting.

"And don't say anything, Keith, because you know I'm right. That lamb thing you make, whatever it is, on the open fire, and they wrote it up in the magazine—"

Keith sat at the bar drinking white wine. He could be brutal when things went wrong in the kitchen but was kind of quiet and bemused otherwise. "Lamb à la Primitive," he said.

"Right. So I ask you. Grease pit? Are you kidding me? And might it not be the cooler thing if we did not respond? If we did not deign to respond."

"I think it's an insult," said the waitress, Charlotte Blonde.

Despite her name Charlotte was a brunette. She had begun waiting tables to pay tuition at the community college in Desmond City, but she got pregnant by a teaching assistant and tuition went up, and now she had an infant daughter and a full-time job.

"And it could add to our cult status," Terry Benton said. "What sort of place would ignore such a sign as if it didn't exist? A cool place, I would think. A place that is very confident of its own value."

"As to the sign, I don't care one way or the other," said Keith Lyon. "I'm not sure we have cult status, but the sign is not an issue to me, because that's not how I get here anyway."

"Well, okay," said Terry. "If we don't have cult status, this might give us one."

And that is why the plywood sign painted with the bitterness of the banned customer still stands on the Lens Lake Road in Shale. It has been changed, though. Now it says:

TWO MILES TO THE
JACK OF DIAMONDS

The judge presiding over the charges against Pierre seemed young and lost in the robe of justice. It was black and slick like a poncho in the rain, and he kept pushing the sleeves up so they would not interfere with his hands.

He was one of those judges who make it a point to know as little as possible about the cases before them. He would state the facts all wrong and rely on the lawyers to set him straight and in general seemed to resent having to deal with so many instances of societal breakdown.

But he was a judge, Pierre thought, and must have aspired to become one, so what had he been expecting?

Naturally, the people in court had problems. Otherwise they wouldn't be in court.

The lawyers responded to the young judge's habitual confusion with deference bordering on sarcasm, laying it on with phrases like "should it please the Court" and "if Your Honor might be directed to the document at his perusal," until you would think that nothing productive ever got done here at all, or, if it did, it was because it had been worked out in advance, as in Pierre's case.

"I have what I take to be a plea agreement," said the judge. "But I will tell you right now that I am neither bound—nor, for that matter, inclined—to accept it."

Pierre's lawyer leaned toward him, bringing along a fog of cologne like the gift shop of a failing hospital. The reflection of the neon lights curved in his large glasses. "Don't worry. He's got to say that. It's just for the people in the cheap seats."

"Being inebriated, the defendant broke up a party," said the judge. "He does not dispute this. He does not express remorse. This is a hostile act disguised as carelessness, and this court doesn't go for that kind of thing. Moreover, if Accelerated Rehabilitation is for exceptional cases—and we agree that it is, so I guess it must be—then—"

"Your Honor, if I might interject," said Pierre's lawyer. "My client did not break up a party. The party, to the best of my knowledge—uh, continued for several hours. And he has plenty of remorse. If he has not expressed it to this point, it is due to the simple fact that no one has asked him or offered a forum in which he might do so."

The judge seized the papers on his desk, looking at one, tossing it aside, looking at another, squinting and scowling. "Where's the bill of particulars?"

"Now, he went *into* a party."

Still shuffling papers, the judge said, as if to himself, "He went into a party. Well, I hate to tell you, but that is not illegal."

"He walked into a house where a party was under way," said the prosecutor. "By virtue of leaving their door unlocked, as one well might while hosting a party, the law-abiding owners of the house became subject to an unwanted incursion which the defendant refused to forego except in his own sweet time."

"Is this true, Pierre?"

"More or less," said Pierre, "but I did leave."

"Was there no violence? What am I thinking of? Was there another case like this one?"

"Let me read to you," the prosecutor continued. "I quote here the police report. 'Asked for why he would not go, subject states he needs a little time and demands they let him do his coin trick or he will not leave.'"

"'For why he would not go. ...'" said the judge.

"Your Honor, if I might footnote that," said Pierre's attorney.

"No, I don't think you might," said the judge. "A coin trick? Is that really why we're here? Am I given to understand we are talking about a coin trick?"

"It's in the affidavit," said the prosecutor. "But I would argue that what he actually did in the house is not pertinent. Only a card trick, perhaps that's so. But does this mean that anyone who breaks into a house will be armored against prosecution provided he insists on performing some—"

"Well now, wait, is it a card trick or a coin trick?" said the judge.

"I'm sorry, you're right; it is a coin trick."

"And would the defendant like to demonstrate this trick for the court?"

"No, Your Honor," said Pierre.

"And, you know, that's probably wise."

The judge found the paper he was looking for, flattened it with the edge of his hand, and signed it.

"I will take the plea," he said. "You know I don't want to, yet by my signature I so order."

Accelerated Rehabilitation had a scientific sound, as if Pierre would rehabilitate faster and faster in an elliptical path until evaporating in a blue flash of pure mental health.

Instead, he entered a counseling class that met once a week in a red Queen Anne house in Desmond City for ten weeks that spring and summer. The counselor had a black and gray ponytail and a gold earring, and he wore pale blue or yellow shirts with voluminous short sleeves, and in general his look seemed calculated to disarm them with its mix of influences.

Pierre found the class slow and insincere. The room where they met had faded green wallpaper with an oppressive pattern of vines, and the box of tissues for the presumed crying could only be considered grotesque. Yet he had no one at all to blame for his being there except himself, and he could not say he didn't learn anything.

One night the class went to an auditorium at the hospital to hear a panel discussion among relatives of people killed in drunk-driving accidents. They spoke of the accidents and how they were told—a phone call, a knock on the door—and of the things left behind that they could not bear to see, and he heard sometimes in their voices a desolation beyond questioning. He thought of the long emptiness of nights that had brought them here to speak reasonably to people who were in essence standing in for the killers. And he did not know how they could do it.

Another time everyone in the class had to select a shrine to a highway fatality and write an essay about it.

There are a number of these makeshift markers on the narrow roads of the Driftless Area. It is hard to give them their due while driving through the normal day. You notice them for a while; then they fade into the scenery as the weather washes their brightness away.

Thus one morning in May, Pierre parked his car up north of Midlothian where a young woman who had attended his high school had died in a crash.

A car driven by a man from Lansville had crossed the center line and sideswiped her car, sending it into a tree. This was three years ago, when she was nineteen years old, and now she would always be that age.

There was a cross decorated with beads, and beneath it people had left perfume bottles and flowers and smooth polished stones. Pierre sat down in the grass with a pad of yellow paper and a pencil. He looked down the road. A string of blackbirds dipped and peeled off in sequence to the east with the red blaze on their wings. It was so quiet he could almost hear the girl's soft and rounded voice from school. But her words were not clear and he had to make them up:

Now you bring flowers and rocks from a rock polisher, when they can help only you. Where were the presents when I was alive? I did get a yellow rose at a dance once but it broke off and I stepped on it while trying to pick it up. Some said I must have been high to trample my rose that way, but I knew there must be some cure from this terrible uneasiness of the young. That time in U.S. History class, for example, when I made the mistake of saying, "Tens of thousands of families gathered up their meager belongings and set out for the Oregon Territory in a single covered wagon." I realize now how it sounded. And you laughed, first some of you and then many, although you knew what I meant, because we had all read the chapter. The laughing hurt, you wouldn't believe how much. So while you drive by now and you might say, How nice, how sad, and think that something has been resolved, I can tell you that it has not. Bring me back, if you want to help. I would be the one who came back. It would be good if one person could. I would speak out at public forums against alcohol and cars. Whatever you want me to say. Out here it's just the birds and the sun and the grasshoppers that zap around in the air. It's strange that this would end up being *my place* when I was only here for such a short time.

"Now, Pierre, I know you have resisted these sessions," said the counselor. "That's been obvious. And you're a bartender. You have a vested interest. But this essay. This essay is just weird."

"Is it?"

"For a number of reasons, yeah. But let me hone in on just one. You say she would speak out against cars."

"Right."

It was the last day of class, and the counselor was meeting with the students one by one to tell them whether they had passed or would be required to take another session. He and Pierre were in the office and the counselor sat behind the desk, worrying his earring and tapping a thick black pen slowly against a clipboard.

"Why cars?"

"Well, I just think that if you took away cars, a lot of the problems that people have with alcohol they wouldn't have. I mean, they might have other problems, but they would be less likely to kill somebody."

"How would they get from place to place?"

"I mean the cars we have now. They're already working on ones that won't crash no matter who's driving—even if nobody's driving."

"Alcohol is the problem with alcohol, Pierre."

"No, I get that. But you have to admit, the transportation system is insane."

"What about you? You weren't driving. Instead, you broke into somebody's house."

"No, I didn't. The door was unlocked. I was just mistaken."

"And still are, Pierre. And still are mistaken," said the counselor. "You might think you're unique, but let me tell you something. You are not. And I don't say this harshly. But you're just like a thousand people who come through this program. You think something outside yourself is going to fix you up. Be it a drink. Be it a drug. Be it a relationship. And then you'll be all right. But you will never be all right. Never. Until you know why you need fixing up in the first place. Does any of this make sense to you?"

"Not really."

The counselor shook his head and picked up the clipboard. "That's about what I figured."

"You're not going to pass me."

"That's correct. My recommendation is one more session. So all I need you to do is sign this document."

He handed the clipboard to Pierre.

"I don't want any more classes."

"That's why this is only a recommendation."

"I don't want to sign it."

"Well, you don't have to."

"Oh. Good."

"I'm asking you to."

"No."

That night the political screamers were on television, screaming about Social Security with their small faces in motion beneath Monster's ashes. Nothing of what they said made any sense at all, yet they said it with such volume and such determination to drown one another out that it became entertaining.

Pierre drank from a green bottle of beer and set it on the floor beside his chair. He tried to think of anyone he knew who worried about Social Security or even gave it a moment's thought.

No, there wasn't anyone.

After a while Pierre fell asleep in his chair. He could sleep anywhere and it did not matter if there was light or sound. If you liked sleep and music, he thought, you could always be happy enough. ...

He dreamed that he and Stella Rosmarin were walking through her house, and though the hallway was dry, all the rooms were flooded. There were Dutch doors, and the top halves stood open so you could see the water that filled the rooms and lapped against the walls.

"Strange, huh? Now look at this," said Stella.

She flicked a wall switch and flames lit up the perimeter of the ceiling. They started in a corner and ran all the way around as if in some unconventional natural-gas setup.

"That doesn't seem right," said Pierre.

Then someone knocked on the door in the dream and the sound got louder until Pierre woke up and found that someone was knocking on his door.

It was Roland Miles, who was married to Carrie Sloan.

"What time is it?" said Pierre.

"I don't know," said Roland. "Eleven-thirty? Twelve? Twelve-thirty?"

"You want a beer?"

"Carrie hit something with her car."

Pierre wiped the sleep from his eyes. "Is she all right?"

"Yeah. The car isn't, though."

"What'd she hit?"

"The car's all messed up on the side. I don't know. A gas pump. The station outside Arcadia."

Pierre got two beers from the refrigerator and they stood in the kitchen and opened them.

"When was this?"

"Couple days ago."

"She hit a gas pump."

"Oh, I don't know. Either that or something near it. She's got to be the most careless person I've ever known in my life. And she wonders why did this happen, why did that happen. She didn't look where she was going. That's how it happened."

"It doesn't sound like anything."

Roland took a drink and his eyes widened, as they do when you're in the middle of a drink and have something to say.

"You wake me up, scare the hell out of me," said Pierre.

"Why are you scared? Do you like her?"

"'Course I like her."

"Yeah, I know you do."

Roland Miles had been all-conference as a halfback for the Shale-Midlothian Lancers but had wrecked his knee in his second year of college and had come back from Nebraska on crutches and proposed to Carrie Sloan.

She said yes and Roland quit college and stayed on in Shale. That was four years ago now. When his knee had healed, he got a job with the parks department, which was a reliable employer of former sports stars.

Pierre could not figure out what Roland's area of responsibility was, and Roland did not seem especially concerned about this himself. He was always driving pickups around with rakes and barrels and sawhorses in the back and no evident requirement to get anywhere.

Roland and Carrie's marriage was famously combative. You would always see them fighting in one parking lot or another. Once they argued with such sarcastic cruelty while playing on opposite sides of a volleyball game that the other players walked away in embarrassment.

They'd each had one affair that Pierre knew of but seemed somehow unlikely to divorce. They were simply two emphatic personalities who were fated to marry and find out what that was like and fight about it.

Pierre and Roland had not been friends that long as they had more or less hated each other in high school; once Roland had even broken Pierre's nose by throwing an elbow at him in football practice.

No one thing cleared up the animosity. It was more that others of their age had moved away or disappeared into parenthood and so they ended up becoming friends through attrition. Plus they were both hunters, and Roland had a sense of honor about hunting that Pierre admired.

A good example would be when some kids from out of town began sneaking up on farmhouses around Shale and picking off tame ducks and geese, and Roland responded by shooting out the windows of their car with bow and arrows while they were in the White Hart bar in Rainville.

Pierre and Roland sat drinking beer with their feet up on Pierre's table.

"I saw Eleanor Carr tonight," said Roland.

This was a woman in town whose son had died several months ago on an island in the Pacific Ocean. It was said to have been a diving accident, but there were also rumors of foul play and nobody knew what the real story was.

"What was she doing?"

"She had these garden shears and she was walking around cutting weeds."

"In her yard?"

"No. The sidewalk. Not even her sidewalk."

"I thought she wouldn't leave the house."

"That's what I thought too."

"What did her son do?" said Pierre.

"Somebody said he might have been working for the government."

"The U.S. government."

"What I heard."

"Maybe it was the Department of Agriculture."

"Yeah, maybe."

"Weights and Measures."

Roland got up and dropped his beer bottle in the galvanized garbage can near the door. "I wouldn't want to die on an island," he said.

"I don't know," said Pierre. "If you have to die, an island wouldn't be so bad."

"I think I'd take a mountain over an island."

Pierre drove out to the lake one Saturday at the end of June. He told himself this was all he meant to do. Just see the lake. And there it was. A wedding was taking place on a houseboat a hundred yards from shore.

The wedding party stood on the boat in their tuxedos and white dresses and the bride's veil and gown moved around like streamers in the wind.

It seemed a little contrived but at least they would always have something to talk about.

He left the beach. The Lake Road took him to the turnoff for Stella's house. Of course this was why he'd come. He drove up into the evergreens where the road was striped with light and shade.

In the clearing of the yard Stella lay in a red bikini and dark glasses on a beach towel in the grass. She sat up and wrapped her arms around her knees when she saw him.

"I knew you would come," she said.

"How?"

"You left your skates."

"Oh, that's right," said Pierre. "I'd forgotten all about them."

Stella's house stood far above the lake, but you could see the north shore through the trees if you knew what you were looking at. In the winter Pierre hadn't noticed how run-down the place was. There were gardens on either side of the house, and they had grown up and fallen into wild tangles of dead vines and new roses.

"Lay out with me awhile," she said.

"I'm not really dressed for it."

She lay back down, and because of the sunglasses he couldn't tell if she was looking at him or not. "Take off as much as you want," she said.

Pierre sat down and pulled off his boots and socks and lay beside her on the grass and closed his eyes.

"You're a modest guy, Pierre," she said.

"I never do this," he said.

"You should. You're pale."

"I used to work on farms. And that's how you got your tan. So I always felt like you should get it by working."

"What strange ideas you have," said Stella. "What did you do on farms?"

"Oh, pick up rocks. Bale hay. The usual farm things."

"And what would you do with these rocks, once you had picked them up?"

The sunlight pressed on his eyelids and the smell of her suntan lotion was warm and summery in the air.

"Throw them in a loader. They come up in the fields and you have to get rid of them or you can't cultivate or something."

"I'm glad you're here," said Stella. "I've been wishing somebody would come by and see how I was doing. Or bring me something they've read and say, 'Have a look at this. It's pretty interesting.'"

"You should get out more," said Pierre.

"Mmm. I know it."

"I just read a book. I could bring it to you."

"Is it interesting?"

"Yeah, but sort of confusing."

"I don't mind that."

"The idea of the book is that time doesn't exist. And everything that ever happened or ever will was here from the start. And even, I think, different versions of what will seem to happen. Or, not here, but somewhere. That's the confusing part. As to where it is exactly. But all at once."

"Do you believe it?"

"I might if I could understand it," said Pierre. "But even while I was reading it, I would turn the page and think, Well, what is that?"

"If not the passage of time."

"Right."

"Yes, bring that, and I'll give it a read."

Pierre opened his eyes. The colors of the grass and sky seemed to vibrate. He propped himself up on one elbow and turned toward her.

"Stella."

"Yes, Pierre."

"Would you like to go somewhere with me sometime?"

"I don't think so," she said. "I need to be here. But you can come back whenever you want."

Then she got up and went into the yellow house and came out carrying the ice skates.

"What did you do to them?"

"Treated the leather, scoured the blades."

"Thank you," said Pierre. "This is something else I owe you for."

"You'd better learn to ride that horse."

Stella lay out a while longer under the sun and then went into the house and put the white robe on and took a string of lights from a cupboard in the kitchen. She arranged them around the bonsai tree on the table and plugged them into the wall with an extension cord. They were small decorative lights in the shape of acorns, with cloth leaves and wire vines attached to the cord between the lights. Some of the lights were shaded light green and others bronze. There was nothing special about them, but she had found them in this house and they helped her to think.

She sat at the table looking at the lights. Sharp at first, they began to blur and pulse as she watched. Her hands lay flat on the table and her breathing slowed and made no sound. She raised her head and closed her eyes but the lights remained in her vision, dimming slowly to darkness. And after a while a series of images began to play in her mind. Some of them she'd seen before, some not. And they always began the same way.

A gloved fist breaks a window
An armchair begins to burn
Walls blister, shatter, and fall
The bed rises, an island in a lake of fire

Now Stella's breath became rapid and broken, and her eyes darted back and forth beneath closed lids.

The Driftless Area at night, ridged and green like
   the folds of a blanket
Pierre skates on the lake
A child's hand draws in blue crayon on a paper plate
A round stone flies through the air
Pierre sits sleeping in the forest, a gun across his legs

She opened her eyes, and wiped her face with the lapel of the robe, and put her hand over her hammering heart.

Carrie Miles sat down at the Jack of Diamonds and dropped her keys on the wood.

"Hey, bartender," she said. "How about a Phillips Screwdriver."

"Well, all right, then," said Pierre.

He made her the drink and gave it to her with a red straw and she drank a third of it right off.

"Guess what," she said. "Roland's shutting me down again."

"Since when?"

"I don't know. A week or so."

"How will you pay for this?"

"Good question. I can't."

"All right."

"Pierre, I swear, if you told me right now I could snap my fingers and make him disappear, I would do it."

"No, you wouldn't."

She set the drink down, raised her hands on either side of her face, and snapped her fingers.

"You'd feel like shit if he really disappeared."

"Well, he's not going to, so it doesn't matter."

"He gets mad, you get mad, it's a vicious cycle."

"He told you he was mad."

"He mentioned something about the car."

"Well, yes. The car. And fuck him. He should marry *that* if he loves it so much."

"That you hit a gas pump."

"No. A cement post at the gas station that's, like, the most deceptive post ever. So he says no money until that's fixed."

"You work. Why don't you just cash your check?"

"Oh, because we have this idiotic system, which I let him talk me into a long time ago. That if one of us makes more than the other, they're entitled to everything the other one makes. But they have to dole it out fairly, of course. Like it's fair that I don't even have five bucks for smokes."

"Never heard of such a thing."

"Well, according to Roland, it's common practice among couples."

"Hell, I'll give you five dollars," said Pierre. "I'll give you fifty."

"Really? You have that much?"

He took his billfold out and opened it. "I've got twenty-three dollars."

"Give me eighteen. I don't want to take all your money."

Pierre counted out eighteen dollars and gave it to Carrie and put his billfold away.

"Something's different about you," she said.

"I graduated from beer school," said Pierre. "That was a rite of passage."

"Hey. Are you in love?"

"Maybe."

"Well, Pierre Hunter. Who with?"

"Don't tell anybody."

"Okay."

"Her name is Stella Rosmarin."

Carrie shook her head. "Why is that name familiar?"

"If you've ever seen her you would remember."

"No. I know what it is. It's a kind of rose. A Rosmarin rose."

*　*　*

Pierre figured it must be a well-known mistake to intervene between a wife and a husband. There were people who did that for a job and they had many years of training, and even they probably only fucked things up half the time.

But none of this was quite real. Roland and Carrie could only talk of their problems, and Pierre could only give advice, in a joking way.

You learned this as a bartender—to humor people in their troubles rather than get all sincere about them. It might have been that the humoring was better anyway. It might let people think things were not so bad and therefore could be worked out. That's what a lot of people came to a bar for anyway.

Of course, what the counselor in beer school had said was that if you drink to make things seem not so bad then those same things will seem worse than ever in the middle of the night when the alcohol burns off.

The counselor would not concede that alcohol had any function at all beyond blind destruction. He made liquor seem like a totally inexplicable historical development. Once in a class Pierre said what seemed obvious to him, that a few drinks enabled people to drop their inhibitions and talk. Even though, yes, there might be—there are—healthier ways to do that. But the counselor reacted as if Pierre had said that a few drinks enabled people to flap their arms and fly like birds.

And everyone in the class sided with the counselor, as they did not want to be held back for another session.

Anyway, the next time Pierre saw Roland—at the Family Lanes bowling alley in Rainville—he told him to quit hoarding the money.

"This is a person who works for a living, in America where, for all its many faults, you do get your money," said Pierre. "She doesn't have five dollars for cigarettes."

"Oh, yeah, the cigarettes," said Roland. "That makes sense as a point of speaking. But who is she smoking with? That's the question."

"Why? Who is she smoking with?"

"How about it's that kid who works on the golf carts, which is why they don't work, because he's standing around breathing smoke on Carrie all the time."

"You're just jealous," said Pierre.

"Of course I am," said Roland. "You know how cute she is."

Pierre made his approach and laid down a green-marbled bowling ball that went on to pick up a seven-ten spare.

"Well, anyway, you owe me eighteen bucks," he said.

The summer came on hot and still. Cars on gravel raised clouds of dust that could be seen for miles, and the sun seemed to develop a personal interest in anyone who moved beneath it.

Boaters and swimmers flocked to Lens Lake and business picked up at the Jack of Diamonds, owing to its quiet and powerful air-conditioning. The dark bar was a good place to be on hot nights, and the red leatherette chairs were gone, replaced by wooden ones from Italy.

One night after work, Pierre went to see Stella. It was around two in the morning when he got there. The treetops framed a column of sky, into which the little house seemed poised to take off, and the moon cast soft blue light on the clapboards.

Pierre shut off the car and walked across the thick and uncut grass. It was still hot, 80 degrees or more. He had no idea whether Stella would welcome him at this time of night. She had said to come back anytime but Pierre had a hard time trusting signs of attraction unless they were totally transparent.

He had left himself an out by bringing her something. It was a model boat he had made. It seemed fairly idiotic, now that he was here and holding the boat in his hands. But at least if she did not want him to stay he could say he only meant to drop it off and be on his way.

The house was dark except for two lights, one on the stove panel in the kitchen and one upstairs. And of course there was no car. Had she cleared out entirely, the place might look exactly this way.

He knocked and after a moment heard a noise from the second floor. The screen window hinged at the top. Stella had pushed it open and was looking down.

"Pierre?" she said.

"Hi," he said. "Is it too late?"

"Come up," she said. "The door's unlocked."

He walked into the house, waited a moment, and climbed the stairs. She stood in the doorway with the light of the room behind her. She wore a little more than she had the last time he saw her but because it was underwear it was more exciting.

Funny how that works, thought Pierre.

"Here," he said. "I made this for you."

She lifted the boat in her hands and closed one eye to look down the hull. "It's beautiful," she said.

"It's a replica of what they call the Gokstad ship," said Pierre. "That's all wood, by the way. Well, except the sail, of course, is cloth."

"This would be the Vikings?"

"Yeah. They think it was a burial ship built around the year nine hundred."

"And you made this?" she said.

"Yeah. You can have it if you want."

"Christ, I love it," she said.

They went into the bedroom, where she set the boat on the dresser. There were sixteen oars on either rail and they were angled downward to enable the model to stand on its own.

"I'll put it here where I can look at it and think of you putting it together."

"It's kind of stupid, but—"

"No, it's not," said Stella. "You don't have to feel that way. Pierre, listen to me. Whatever is bad, you didn't cause it. You can feel good if you want to."

She raised her hands with fingers apart as if she had counted ten things. "Wouldn't that be better? Isn't that what you want?"

He laced his fingers in hers. "I want you," he said. "And there, I've said it."

Still holding Pierre's hands, Stella drew her arms back, pulling the two of them together, and she pressed his hands to the small of her back.

It was very graceful, how she did that. He could feel the ribbed cloth of her undershirt and the hem of it and the warm skin beneath.

"You're the one I've been waiting for," she said.

A woman had once told Pierre that men mistake sex for love, or maybe it was love for sex, he could not remember how it went, and maybe that only proved her point. But he thought there should be love in it, or created by it, and maybe this was why he hadn't slept with too many people.

Of course it wasn't always what it could be. Sometimes there was a disappointing sense of a favor being granted, and reluctantly at that, a sense of calculation and separation, and this reduced the experience from ecstatic union to a hybrid of gymnastics and accounting, and all in all it could be kind of tense and gloomy.

With Stella it was not like that. She was wild and lovely and drew no line between what she gave and what she took. She wanted and Pierre wanted what they were after equally, or sometimes one a little more, and sometimes the other, and the differences gave way to creativity rather than isolation.

And what were they after? It was not only the good feeling of friction and slide, though that was much of it. Maybe there was a time before individual minds when sensation fell on the world and all knew it the same. It was something like that. To find that time and live it one night. To join together, as in the wedding vows. It was like the word that Pierre had spoken of that time he was drunk—which time, there were so many—the word that would say everything, and the word was the sound of breathing.

They made love all through the night. It was hot in the room and then cooler as the early morning drifted in the windows, until at last they shivered under the covers, played out and a little deranged. There was a light on, a standing lamp with an orange shade. The wiring was bad and it kept going on and off. Sometimes it would stay on for a while and then again it would strobe, and the light in its changeable modes seemed to urge them on. And they would sleep, but lightly, each with the awareness of the other held close.

Once they woke and they were still together and she lay on him with her hands touching his face and her head beneath his chin.

"So, what are you doing this summer?" she said, and he could feel the vibration of her voice in his chest.

They laughed. She rose on her golden arms and looked at him.

"You mean like a vacation?" he said.

"Yeah, maybe."

"I usually go to California in August. A cousin of mine lives out there with her family. But I don't know if I will this year."

"Why not?"

"Well, see, I hitchhike."

"But you have a car."

"It would never make it. It's too far. And you can actually go faster without one, because you don't have to stop. But I don't know. I'm twenty-four now. Getting kind of old for it."

"Twenty-four is nothing."

"And besides, you're here."

"You should do whatever you were going to do," said Stella. "Don't not go for me. And then you can come back and tell me the stories."

"I've wanted this since the day we met," said Pierre. "Even on the day we met."

"You were so cold."

"I've forgotten."

"I remember everything."

"That's quite a lot."

"Some things I'd just as soon forget."

"This helps, though, doesn't it?"

"Yes, because it's only us."

"And who are we again?"

"A guy and a gal, lost together in this funky world."

"How pretty you say that."

"We should take it slow," she said. "Really slow—like this—until it's just unbearable. ..."

At around five o'clock the light began to seep into the room and the birds to sing in tentative phrases as if to find out who else was awake. Pierre got up and shut off the erratic lamp, and as he did so he got a shock that leaped all the way to his shoulder. He walked back to the bed, kneading his knuckles, and then they went to sleep and did not get up until the afternoon.

"I heard you had one cart," said Roland Miles. "Carrie seen you in the store."

"So?"

"Well, you know what that means."

They were up on the stone tower in the state forest behind the Jack of Diamonds. Roland was patching the mortar between the stones where it had cracked to white ash and fallen out, and Pierre was leaning on the wall and looking out over the country.

"Two people, one cart," said Roland.

"No, what does it mean?" said Pierre.

"That you're living together."

"What if we are?"

"Are you?"

"No."

"Okay, then."

"I took her to get some groceries."

"How kind of you. Carrie said you were in the hair care aisle and looking pretty goddamned cozy."

"She should've come over."

"Well, you know—you don't want to interrupt people when they're deciding which conditioner gives that all-over shiny feeling."

"I like her."

"That's good," said Roland. "You should like someone. It's the way people are. And she likes you?"

"Seems that way."

"Why?"

the drawings. So he jumped to his feet, took the lucky rock from the pocket of his coat, wound up, and threw the rock at the truck.

Sometimes things happen that seem to defy the second law of thermodynamics, which states that all systems move toward disorder. Once Pierre had dropped a lighter on the sidewalk, and it landed standing up. Another time, lying in bed with Stella, he asked what she would do if he could toss a quarter across the room and into a coffee cup sitting on the dresser by the Gokstad ship, and she told him, and he threw the coin, and it went in the cup.

And now the pickup began to move, tires spinning for a hold on the pavement, but it didn't matter, because the rock in its flight seemed to know what it was meant to do, and it followed a low arc and tailed off, going through the window frame and hitting the driver. The truck went on up the ramp for a short while, losing speed, and then veered west and down a grassy embankment, where it rolled for a while, missed some trees, hit another one, and stopped.

Spellbound, Pierre walked down the bank and through the trees to the truck, where the driver lay partly on the seat and partly in the foot well under the dashboard. Pierre watched him awhile to make sure he was breathing, though he had no idea what he would have done if he were not.

"I'm not sure," said Pierre. "There's some deer down here."

"What are they doing?"

"Just walking around. Now they're running."

"Any fawns?"

"I don't think so."

"They're probably near, they usually are.... I'm not saying you're on the bottom of the barrel. I'm sure you would stand out to somebody, just given how many people there are, and the laws of probability."

"Yep," said Pierre. "It's a mystery."

"Well, don't listen to me."

"I'm not."

"I can see that."

Pierre had learned something in college that he always remembered, and this was that everything that succeeds creates the conditions for its own demise.

A professor with a prematurely bent posture and white beard had said this about an ancient kingdom that had disappeared, and Pierre thought it was true of many things.

A simple example would be a fire, which burns the fuel that feeds it and goes out. Supposedly this would even happen to the sun. Or a hero, who rights some great wrong and finds that his services are no longer needed.

It was the only philosophy he had, although he was not sure it was philosophy. It meant that nothing sufficiently good or bad can last. The only things that might last are things that make no difference.

Yet it was like Pierre to magnify simple questions into large abstractions about which nothing could be done. All he meant in thinking of this formula for dissolution was that if he and Stella moved in together, they would put an end to the living apart that made them want to live together in the first place.

So he never raised the issue, and neither did Stella. They spent many nights at her hilltop house and one at his apartment in Shale before he left on his trip to California. These nights and mornings seemed so luminous and urgent as to exist separately from the rest of his life. It was as if they were beginning the world from nothing every time they met. Where had he been all this time? That was the question that went through his mind when he and Stella were together. And where was he now?

FIVE

Pierre had never really got a bad ride. The worst that happened was that a driver would share an unexpectedly powerful strain of grass and play some song like "Tecumseh Valley" and Pierre would become sort of comatose. Much of the music was old, as were most of the drivers, who remembered a time when the roads were jammed with people thumbing rides.

He made fantastic time. The hitchhiker may appear carefree and open to experience, but in Pierre's case this was deceptive. He got ruthless on the road, greedy for miles. He did not have to be anywhere in a hurry, but he hurried anyway.

He remembered some of the people who had given him rides—a quiet, serious man who went from track to track gambling on horses, another man with a rusted tub of crawdads in the backseat, a woman in a tan Karmann Ghia who laughed beautifully and lit up a metal hash pipe, winking like Santa's sexy niece as the white smoke curled around her face.

But in each case the ride had ended and he had gone on—he did not attend the crawdad bake (or fry, or however the crawdads would be prepared), or learn to interpret a racing form, or spend the night with the hash smoker.

Sometimes he thought it would be better if he had done these things. Not that he could have done them all. Only the gambler had offered. But there may have been signals that Pierre in his transient nature had missed. To turn your life on a dime seemed to him the essence of American thought. But he had never been able to do so until now.

He made Utah in two nights, and there he met a tragic sort of woman in a mountain town. She was thirty years old or so and drinking in the bar of the dark and worn-down hotel where he had checked in for the night.

She'd had some hard times. Something begins to fade from the eyes after too much of anything. She had thick dry reddish hair and white scars on either side of her face as if she had been attacked by a bear.

In fact, she said, she'd done this with her own fingernails one time after going too many days on speed. Pierre did not know what to say to that, but she smiled and nodded, as if the pain had faded, leaving only a sort of impersonal amazement.

They danced in the bar and then, wanting to see the town, Pierre walked her home, to the house where she said she lived with her grandmother. The house was close to the newly paved road that fell away from the town. The door was locked, and she knocked and called out, but nothing happened.

"She does this if I come home late," she said. "But there's a ladder in the garage. Come on. You can help me carry it."

So they went in the garage and she turned on a light and looked around. There was a big yellow Cadillac but no ladder that they could find.

She stood with her hands in her back pockets and looked all around the garage. "Clever," she said. "She must have taken the ladder in the house. Good one, Grandma. That's thinking ahead for you. This is kind of a game we play."

"Why don't you come back to the hotel?" said Pierre. "You can sleep in my room."

"Oh, no," she said. "I don't swing that way."

"You don't have to swing any way," said Pierre. "You can stay there, that's all."

"Really? You would do that for me? You must be a religious kind of guy. 'Cause what I normally do if I can't get in is sleep in the Cadillac."

"Well, you don't want to do that."

"No, that's for sure."

So they went back to the hotel and stayed the night, all on the straight and narrow, she in the bed and Pierre in a chair with a blanket.

"And how are you doing over there?" she said.

"Very well, thanks."

"You might be interested to know I'm off the crank now."

"That's good."

"And here's a promise I made to myself. That someday, when I find a pile of cash, I'll take it to a plastic surgeon and I'll say, 'Make these scars go away.'"

"They probably can."

"Oh, these days? It's a snap, I bet. They probably do it all the time."

"The cash is the tricky part," said Pierre.

"I think it will happen, though. I can just see it."

"If you can see it, you can be it."

"Where'd you hear that?"

"Beer school."

"So you've abused substances too," she said.

"Oh, many a time."

"Do you think it's true?"

"What?"

"If you can see it, you can be it."

"No. What time is it?"

"Two o'clock."

"For example, you can see a llama," said Pierre. "But you couldn't be one."

"That's taking it pretty literal."

"I'm going to sleep now."

"You have passed your test," she said.

"I didn't know I was taking one."

"You didn't ask for anything or come jumping all over me. You were true to what you said, and you're sleeping in some scuzzy chair. I admire that."

"You can't spend the night in your grandmother's car."

"Hey, I got news for you. That wasn't even her house."

"It wasn't."

"Uh-uh."

"What if there had been a ladder?"

"That would have been interesting, wouldn't it?"

"What are you, crazy?"

"Yeah, I guess. Probably pretty crazy."

"Are you going to sleep now?"

"Yeah."

"Good night."

"No. You know what? I'm giving you something."

She rummaged in her purse and then leaned way out from the bed, with one hand on the floor, and handed him a round yellow stone about the size of a tennis ball and covered with small depressions like the moon.

"Thanks," he said.

"It's my lucky rock," she said. "I found it in a quarry. I think it was made by heat or something."

"You should keep it."

"No, it's too heavy. I've been looking for somebody to give it to. It has a good feel to it. You'll like it. Go ahead, throw it up and catch it. You'll see what I mean."

"Yeah," said Pierre. "It's kind of sandy."

"Didn't I tell you?"

And for the rest of the trip, all the way to the coast and back, he carried the rock in the pocket of his safari coat, and he would throw it up and catch it while watching the road for rides.

Pierre's cousin and her family lived in a small house in northern California with peeling redwood trees growing in the back, and they would pitch a tent in the yard for Pierre to sleep in.

His cousin owned a company that made custom skateboards endorsed by an apparently famous skateboarder Pierre had not heard of, and her husband had a repair shop specializing in Saabs, and he drove old Saabs and thought Saabs were about the greatest thing.

Their children were good souls and backgammon prodigies who would beat Pierre almost every time they played. He thought he was a fair backgammon player but he was nothing compared to these children, who were five, seven, and nine years old.

Even the youngest had a keen understanding of how to block, and when to hit blots or leave them alone, and when to double. It was extraordinary.

Pierre stayed with them one week and it never got crowded or uncomfortable, on account of the tent. They would chop wood for their winter supply and go to the ocean near Big Sur, where the children ran through the tidal pools.

His cousin had an unorthodox style with an ax. She would not toss the blade to the side and swing, as most do, but begin with the ax hanging motionless down her back and bring it up and over her head with gathering speed. And in this way, though slender and not very tall, she could split blocks that Pierre would barely dent.

His cousins had the sanest family life that Pierre had ever known. The kids called him Uncle Pierre, and the day before he headed up the coast, they drew their faces on paper plates and gave them to him so he would remember what they looked like.

So now he had the rock, and he had the paper plates, and everything was in place for what would happen next, although Pierre did not know what this would be, or even that it would be anything.

It happened when he was nearly home. He got a little careless as he often did at the end of the journey. At a truck stop in Minnesota, he took a ride from a man in a battered sky-blue pickup who asked if he would split the gas money.

Both the shape that the truck was in and the driver's request for money might normally have made Pierre wait for another ride. Sharing the cost was fair in theory but, from what he had seen, drivers who made a point of asking up front tended toward the mercenary.

As for the truck, the panels were dented and scraped, the dashboard was delaminating, and there was no glass in the back window. But it was late afternoon and he had only 125 miles to go, so Pierre took the ride.

The driver was a large man with long hair in a shade between yellow and white. Of Pierre's age or maybe a few years older, he wore a green Boy Scout shirt with the arms sawed off at the shoulders and a royal blue insignia identifying him as a DISTINGUISHED EXPERT, though in what field it did not say, and probably the shirt had not belonged to the driver when the award was earned anyway.

He had a round and sunburned face and jutting brow, and he would not look Pierre in the eyes but always seemed to be thinking of some other situation, and sometimes he appeared laid-back and at other times, for no reason, a look of alarm would flicker across his face.

And as they went along the driver said he was going down to San Antonio, to help his brother, who had found a lot of money in a car wash. Or rather than saying it he yelled it, or nearly so, to be heard above the highway sound that rolled through the missing window.

"How much is it?" said Pierre.

"Thousands. Tens of thousands."

"And somebody left it in a car wash."

"So he tells me."

"What is it, drug money?"

"Well, we don't know. But ill-gotten gains of some kind. It was in a paper sack from a grocery store."

"What if whoever left it wants it back?"

Pierre was only making conversation. The story sounded made up, though it was not that unusual for something you would hear while hitchhiking.

"Yeah, my brother's kind of worried about that aspect of it," said the driver, with his hair dancing around in the back draft of the missing window. "But once he gets it to San Antonio those bastards can't touch him."

"I thought it was in San Antonio."

"That's what I mean."

Pierre's backpack was then riding along in the bed of the pickup, in violation of a fundamental rule of hitch-hiking, which is not to get separated from anything you don't want to lose.

The end of the ride showed the reason for the rule. When they came to the turnoff for the highway that Pierre would take east the seventy miles to Shale, the driver went halfway up the exit ramp and stopped there on the shoulder.

"Why don't you pull up to the stop sign. I'll get out there," said Pierre.

"No, thanks, this is fine."

Pierre looked across at the driver, thinking he had not understood. "You've got to go there anyway."

"Yeah, I don't care."

"Just right up here," said Pierre.

The driver turned in his seat, set his back to the door, and kicked Pierre in the shoulder.

"Get the fuck out of my truck," he said.

"Well, okay, but it seems goddamn small after I gave you gas money."

"And don't forget your stuff."

Once he said that Pierre saw his mistake. Still, there was nothing to do but get out. He opened the door and began to step down and the truck took off, throwing him on the pavement.

But then the driver made a mistake of his own. Instead of leaving as fast as he could, he stopped a little ways off, and looked back through the glassless window, and yelled something. Pierre could not tell what, but it seemed to end with the word *fool*, which was hard to argue with under the circumstances.

The backpack held nothing of value, but Pierre hated the thought of the thief getting the paper plates with the drawings. So he jumped to his feet, took the lucky rock from the pocket of his coat, wound up, and threw the rock at the truck.

Sometimes things happen that seem to defy the second law of thermodynamics, which states that all systems move toward disorder. Once Pierre had dropped a lighter on the sidewalk, and it landed standing up. Another time, lying in bed with Stella, he asked what she would do if he could toss a quarter across the room and into a coffee cup sitting on the dresser by the Gokstad ship, and she told him, and he threw the coin, and it went in the cup.

And now the pickup began to move, tires spinning for a hold on the pavement, but it didn't matter, because the rock in its flight seemed to know what it was meant to do, and it followed a low arc and tailed off, going through the window frame and hitting the driver. The truck went on up the ramp for a short while, losing speed, and then veered west and down a grassy embankment, where it rolled for a while, missed some trees, hit another one, and stopped.

Spellbound, Pierre walked down the bank and through the trees to the truck, where the driver lay partly on the seat and partly in the foot well under the dashboard. Pierre watched him awhile to make sure he was breathing, though he had no idea what he would have done if he were not.

Then he got his pack from the truck bed and went up and pulled the latch beneath the steering wheel and opened the hood. His thought was to tear out the ignition wires, but their location was not as obvious as he had hoped. But while surveying the various webs of wires he saw a package that had been secured with duct tape behind the battery.

He pulled off the tape and took the package from the engine well. It was a paper sack, folded over and bound with more tape, and when he got that off and opened the bag he found that it was full of faded green bills bundled by ink-stained rubber bands.

Pierre thought for a short while and then opened his pack and pushed everything down and laid the sack of money in on top. Then he went back to the sleeping driver and pulled the keys out of the ignition and flung them into a bean field and walked away.

He put the pack on his shoulders and went up the exit ramp. He walked for several miles under the light-banded sky and eventually a man driving a Royal Crown truck stopped to give him a ride.

SIX

WHEN THE driver of the pickup woke it was dark outside, and the light on the roof of the truck was on. A woman had hold of his foot and was shaking it.

He was upside down with his head under the dashboard on the passenger side and his feet up by the steering wheel. His head hurt. He put his hand to his hair and it was matted like straw.

"You've been in an accident," said the woman.

"Yeah," he said. "What time do you have?"

"It's about nine o'clock. I was on my way home from the cemetery. I put flowers down, you know. But today I got busy and didn't get to it until late. But I don't feel right till I do it, so—anyway. Do you have anything broken, do you think? Not that you'd necessarily know. I'm sure glad I stopped."

He reached up to open the passenger door and he crawled out and came around to the driver's side where the woman was standing.

"Why did you stop?" he said.

"Oh, my husband. He drives the wrecker in town and he's supposed to pick up any cars and tow them in should they be wrecked or abandoned. So anyway I thought I better see what the deal was because I didn't want him making the trip for nothing. What's your name?"

"Bob Johnson," he said.

That name was made up. He might have come up with something better but he was not thinking very clearly. His name was Shane Hall.

He noticed then that the hood was up and he didn't like the look of that. So he walked up beside the truck and felt around behind the battery. He doubted that the money would have fallen out on impact, but he got down and looked around and under the truck.

"What are you doing, Mr. Johnson?" said the woman. "Do you want me to call someone?"

"No, I'm all right," said Shane. "But there was someone else. I remember now. In the truck. I don't know where he is."

"Maybe he was thrown out. I've heard of that happening. I'd better go call someone. I don't like this at all."

"No, help me, now. We can't panic. You look around here, I'll look back in the trees."

Shane walked up to the woman's car parked on the shoulder of the ramp, but she had locked the door. So he returned to the truck and got behind the wheel but the keys were gone.

"This isn't fair," he said.

He saw the rock on the seat, picked it up, and stared at it.

"I don't find anyone," she said.

Shane got out of the truck with the rock in his hand.

"Yeah, me neither," he said. "Listen, I need to take your car. I have to go the doctor's. I think you're right about that. So let's have the keys."

"You're in no shape to drive," she said. "I wouldn't be surprised if you have a concussion. I'll drive you into town and we'll get the ambulance in no time. I know where there is one."

"Give me the keys to your car. Don't make me hit you with this rock."

"You would do that?"

"Yeah, I would."

"But how will I get home?"

"I don't know. Christ, figure it out. You'll walk, I imagine. Why is everyone always expecting me to take them somewhere?"

She got her ring of keys out and took the one for the car off the ring and gave it to him. "What about this other guy, that was in the truck."

"He's dead. He doesn't know it yet but he will."

"Oh, my."

"Yes. I know. That's what I'm trying to tell you."

Shane drove the woman's car up the ramp and turned east onto the highway. It was a very smooth ride—much better than the truck with the shot-out window. Plastic trays of dead flowers were on the seat and he picked them up and threw them out the window and watched in the mirror as they bounced and broke apart on the asphalt.

Simple as his mission seemed, he knew it would not be simple at all unless he happened on the hitchhiker along the highway. He had not really caught his name although it thought it might have been Pete or some lame name like that.

He drove for several hours. The flat country gave way to hills, and the road climbed, and valleys opened on either side, and in the valleys there were towns every so often.

To go into any one of them and start looking around would be pointless, as Shane well knew, lonely little places hunkered in with streetlamps marking the passage of the nothing night.

Shane was torn between ignoring the stupid thing he had done and berating himself for it. He had waited around like a fool, no question about it, but who could have predicted the hitchhiker would have such an arm, or something to throw?

He had seen the rock on its way. All he would have had to do was duck, or even stay still, for he had turned his head and hit the gas, and the truck had moved, it must have, which meant that the throw would have gone wide had he done nothing.

Everything had happened exactly as it had to for Shane to lose the money—it seemed both inevitable and ridiculous—and after that all was lost in stony sleep until the cemetery woman woke him by shaking his foot.

When he got to the river at the border he knew that he had gone too far, so he went down into a town and stopped at a bar on piers over the river. He sat drinking beer and looking out at the dark plane of water with boat lights moving over it.

The worst thing was that he had put the money at risk for nothing, some dope's backpack of junk; it was galling as hell as he considered it.

"Penny for your thoughts," said the waitress, as she brought him another draw.

"Just put the beer down and get away from me."

He stopped at a pay phone on his way out of the bar. He called a guy he knew in Chartrand, forty miles to the south, and told him he needed a place to stay.

As the evening had turned cooler, he picked up a jacket and hat from hooks on the wall, and outside he put them on and went on his way.

"So this is it," Pierre said.

He put the sack of money on Stella's table and she pulled it over and looked inside.

"What will you do with it?"

"I don't know. Maybe invest it."

"At so many percent."

"Yeah. Not really."

"Because she said. This woman you met," said Stella. She had her hair in two long ponytails and she wore a blue denim shirt with mother-of-pearl buttons.

"If she found a lot of cash. Her words."

"And the rock."

"Yeah. She gave me the rock."

"Well, I don't know, Pierre. I guess it's meant to be."

"But even if it isn't. Say she didn't know about the money. Because it isn't humanly possible. Why not give it to her anyway?"

"Just that she might throw it away."

"Everybody who has money might throw it away," said Pierre. "A lot of them do. But nobody ever worries about it unless somebody who doesn't have any is about to get some."

"And then you'll be free of it," said Stella. "I like that. It's Robin Hood and yet it's not."

"Well, I did take it. Is it stealing? I'm not sure what it is. When you take money someone stole, while he's also trying to steal from you. What is that?"

"That is the way it goes."

"I mean it's not like I wanted it."

"I don't fault what you did, Pierre. You followed your instincts. Does he know where to find you?"

"No."

"Because he will try."

"You think so."

"I'm certain of it. This is probably all the money he had in the world. Or maybe he owes it to somebody. He wakes up, the money's gone, he can't drive. What would you do?"

"Well, he won't know to look in Utah."

"Do you have an address?"

"I don't. I thought I would call the bar I met her in. Or the hotel."

"Did you sleep with her?"

"No."

"It's all right if you did."

"I didn't. I'd tell you. That's why she gave me the rock."

"Okay, good. Now, do you have any weapons?"

"For what?"

"To defend yourself, I suppose."

"I have a twelve-gauge and a rifle, but I'm not planning to use them."

"But what if you need to?" she said. "It's like the rock. You weren't planning on that, either, but it's a good thing you had it."

"A rock is one thing."

"I'm not sure you understand," said Stella. "Do you see this? This is a *fortune.*"

"I need a cardboard box."

She went and came back with a box in which Habenaria bulbs had been shipped. This seemed ideal because no one inclined to steal from the mail would get excited about flowers.

That night at the Jack of Diamonds, Pierre made some calls to the town of Cassins Finch, Utah, and got the woman on the phone.

"Hey, I remember you," she said. "We were looking for a ladder that night."

Pierre leaned over the bar with pen and paper. "Give me your address. I'm sending you something."

"Bad or good?"

"Good."

"I don't want the rock back."

"It's not the rock."

* * *

Shane followed the river south and arrived around midnight in Chartrand, a city laid out along the water and one that had a reputation for shadiness because of its unusual concentration of dealers and fences and bookmakers. The man he went to see was called Ned Anderson, short for Edmund.

Ned's trade was partly legal and partly not. He ran a car rental place at the regional airport and sold methamphetamines in the form of little white pills. It was a solid and quiet living that he made from the two enterprises. He could have cleared more selling modern drugs but believed that the white cross drew less attention from cops and competitors.

He had the speed flown in from California, bypassing the fly-by-night meth labs, which he considered shabby and unreliable. The rental operation provided a clandestine freight depot for the speed. Ned thought of himself as a regular businessman and made it a point to donate to charities and political candidates.

Ned lived in a ranch house in a low-slung neighborhood where only the mailboxes were ornate. Shane knocked on the door and was ushered in by a woman with a red wool blanket drawn around her shoulders. Without a word she led him back to the kitchen, where she took her place at an oval table of quarter-sawn oak.

There she and Ned and two others were trying out a batch of amphetamines. They crushed the tablets with the edges of coins and inhaled the powder through rolled dollars. With the money and the white dust on the sturdy table, they looked like employees in the last days of banking.

Ned stood at the head of the table, tall and imposing with a big stomach that seemed to symbolize power rather than excess weight, though that's what it was. His hair and eyebrows were wavy and dark red and his head tilted forward with a serious squint to his eyes. He wore a coarse gray suit and a blue tie loose at the collar.

"I got a car out here you should get rid of," said Shane.

"Why don't you get rid of it?" said the woman who had brought him in. She had black glossy bangs that came down to the top of her eyelids.

"I'll leave it where it is if that's where you want it," said Shane.

"Here, here, let's not fight," said Ned. "What do you want done with it?"

"It's your town, you decide," said Shane.

"Get the car out of here," said the woman in the red blanket.

"We haven't been introduced," said Shane.

"This is Luanne Larsen," said Ned.

"Pleased to meet you. I'm Shane."

"We know who you are."

Ned introduced the two others. One was Jean Story, who sat with her arms folded in a shirt of light gray cotton and smiled fiercely with hard green eyes. The other was Lyle Wood-Mills, whom Shane had met before, a mechanic who made deliveries for Ned and coordinated his network of dealers. In Shane's view, Lyle was a complainer, who viewed any given situation as a nest of negative implications for Lyle, but Ned considered him capable and even essential to both his businesses.

"Join us," said Ned. "This stuff isn't bad."

"It's fresh," said Jean, rubbing her nose with the back of her hand. "It has a certain quality."

"I wouldn't go that far," said Luanne. "It's all right. I don't love it."

"I think I'll clean up and go to bed," said Shane. "We have something to talk about, but we can do that tomorrow."

"What kind of thing?" said Ned.

Shane went to the refrigerator and got a wedge of Swiss cheese and stood at the counter slicing it with a knife. "Money," he said.

"What happened to your head?" said Jean.

"I was in a car accident."

"Get the car out of here," said Luanne. "He can't stay here. Tell him, Ned."

"Leave it, Luanne," said Ned. "I owe him. Shane's troubles are my troubles."

"Yeah, they probably will be," she said. "I know. He

went to jail on your behalf or some stupid thing like that."

"Never mind what," said Ned.

"I didn't go to jail," said Shane.

"Lyle, move the car, will you," said Ned.

"Where?"

"Take it that place we took that other one. And get the plates. Jean, you follow Lyle."

"Will do, Ned."

"It's a Buick," said Shane. "Where do I go?"

"There's a room upstairs with an exercise bike. You can have that."

"I work out there," said Luanne.

"I wonder if there's one thing you wouldn't have to fight me on," said Ned. "It could be anything. I've been waiting. I hope it appears one day."

Shane went upstairs and took a shower and lay on a couch in the exercise room with the coat he'd stolen from the bar as a blanket. Sometime later he woke to find Jean in the room. She stood by the door in the gray cotton shirt, which seemed to float in the darkness.

"We took care of your car," she said.

"Thanks."

"Ned said come tell you."

"All right, then."

"And see if you want anything else."

"I'm all set."

"Any old thing."

"Oh, I get it."

"Yeah, I seen the lightbulb come on."

"What kind of place is this?"

"It's Ned Land. You want to get laid?"

"I guess, if you want to."

"Not especially."

"This is real seductive."

"I know, my pulse is racing."

"Skip it. You don't have to. Ned isn't anything."

"He's my boss."

"Where?"

"The rent-a-car."

"Don't you have your own place?"

"Do you mind if I smoke?"

"Go ahead."

She sat on the arm of the couch. Her lighter was one of those little blow-torch numbers that hiss and emit a spear of blue fire. She tilted her head back and blew smoke at the exercise bicycle. "My hubby and me had a falling-out."

"How come?"

"He's got a girlfriend. You know. So I said either she goes or I go. So anyway, I went. And then Ned said it was okay here."

"When was this?"

"I don't know. A year ago, maybe."

"Do you and Ned … you know. …"

"Oh, God, no. He's too old for me. 'Course he's too old for Luanne too, but Luanne lives in her own space. You saw what she's like. Everything to look out for Ned, to the point where she almost despises him."

"So what do you do, sit around doing speed the whole time?"

"Not really. I mean, I'll have it, it makes me kind of happy, but I'm not a fanatic about it."

"So why'd you stay?"

She thought the question over, staring into the room. "I think I'm depressed," she said. "Maybe that's it. And this is a good place for that. No one tells you to get out of it. We keep the shades down in the windows. We watch the vids. I ride to work with Ned. It isn't so bad."

"What would you do if you had to find someone? And you didn't know their name."

"I don't know. Probably look on the Internet."

"He lives north of here."

"That's not much to go on. What else?"

"Just got back hitchhiking from California."

She took the cigarette from her lips and gestured with it and nodded. "Now, see, *that*," she said. "That is something you could work with."

"On the Internet."

"Well, no. Just talking to someone. Unless he has a blog."

"What's that?"

"An online diary," said Jean. "Do you think he might?"

"I don't know. I fucking doubt it."

"Yeah, probably not."

"You could help me," said Shane. "People tell women things they wouldn't tell men. Or if you have contacts up there. I'll pay you."

"How much?"

Shane thought for a minute. "Couple hundred. If I find him."

"Yeah, I don't know. I'll sleep on it."

"Stay a minute."

"Yeah? Why?"

"I want you to sit on my back."

"Is this a sexual thing for you?"

"No. I've always had problems with it. I think I hurt it when my truck went off the road."

"Okay."

Shane lay on his stomach with his head turned to the side and Jean sat on his back. She reclined and rested her arms on the top of the couch.

"How's that?" she said.

"Good. Much better."

"What did you do for Ned? That he was alluding to."

"Why do you want to know? You wouldn't want to sit on my back anymore."

"It can't be that bad."

"It's right up there."

"Tell me."

"I burned a house down," said Shane. "It was a job for hire. Supposed to be empty. But there was somebody in it and she didn't get out."

"Wow."

"Told you."

"That *is* bad."

"I know it."

"Who was she?"

"I don't know. She was watching the house."

"And you didn't know?"

"No," said Shane.

"God."

"And what do you do?"

"What?"

"For Ned."

"Oh. Nothing. I bump people up."

"What's that?"

"They come in, they want the economy car, I—and she died? This person?"

"Yeah. It was a couple years ago."

"Did Ned know?"

"No. We all thought it was empty. He said it was my fault. That I should have known. But what were you saying? The people come in—"

"And I just—I just bump them up to something more than they want. A different car."

"How do you do that?"

"It's easy. Talk low, talk slow. Wear a gold necklace with your shirt open a couple buttons."

"And then what?"

"That's it."

"Just in the appearance."

"Yeah. Everyone knows this."

"The men."

"Men, women ... businessmen, it makes no difference," said Jean. "Of course it doesn't always work. But I think most people kind of want to be bumped up anyway."

One Thursday night, the Reverend John Morris of the Church of the Four Corners came into the Jack of Diamonds and sat at the bar to have supper. He did this most every week. He would have the venison and onions, or the red snapper with grilled tomatoes, and red wine with his food and Calvados after.

The pastor liked to eat and drink, yet he was old and troubled. He had absorbed the problems of the congregation and some of his own. His wife had left him several years ago for a younger minister, and though she had returned after a few months, he was never quite the same. The past was in his eyes, and he walked stiff-shouldered and full of regret.

"Hi, Pastor," said Pierre. He had two glasses in either hand and slotted them up to dry.

"You know that little white convertible your dad used to drive?" said John Morris.

"Sure. The MGA."

"Sweet car."

"It was."

"Whatever happened to it?"

"I don't know. It got sold when the house got sold."

"How come you didn't get any of that stuff?"

"It was part of the estate. I didn't really get involved in it."

"Well, I think I saw it the other day."

"Oh, yeah? Where?"

"It was up for sale where I get my car worked on."

"I wouldn't mind seeing it."

"Well, it's not there anymore. It went out the next day."

"Too bad," said Pierre.

"Yeah. I saw it and I thought, Pierre should have this."

"He rebuilt it himself. I remember he had it all taken apart to where it didn't even look like a car. There were wires laying all over the place."

"Well, anyway, here's the keys."

John Morris put them down on the bar. It was the same key ring too, a little brass snaffle bit.

"You bought it?" said Pierre.

"It's yours. I heard you were hitchhiking again and then I saw the car and it all made sense."

They went out of the bar and to the edge of the lot by the brook where the car was. Pierre walked beside it, trailing his hand down the long subtle curve of the fender.

"Are you serious, John? What'd you pay for it?"

"Not that much. I baptized the guy's kids so he cut me a deal."

After the bar closed, Pierre and the chef, Keith Lyon, took the car for a drive. They went up to the Grade and drank a couple beers and smoked a joint.

"You owe that minister," said Keith.

"Probably I should go to church now or something."

"A time or two wouldn't hurt."

"Hey, listen. Somebody might be after me."

"For what?"

"I took something they had."

Keith opened the glove box. "Light still works," he said. "Well, I guess you could give it back."

"I don't have it."

"What is it?"

"Seventy-seven thousand dollars."

"Really. That's different, isn't it? What did you do with so much money?"

"Gave it away."

"Stole it and gave it away."

"No," said Pierre. "I didn't steal it. I wouldn't call it that. It was more like gambling, but he didn't understand how much he was betting."

"You're going to have to tell me what we're talking about."

They got out of the car and walked to the edge of the Grade and stood throwing rocks down at the water as Pierre explained what happened.

"So what you're saying," said Keith. "This guy got your clothes, and you got enough money to buy a house."

"Well, no," said Pierre, "because I got the clothes back."

"It was not his day, was it?"

"No."

"What's his name?"

"I don't know. Long-haired guy. Big guy."

"What the fuck, you hit him with a rock?"

"Yeah."

"Can you draw?"

"Some."

And this was true. One year in the fall after Pierre finished college he had gone on an illustration kick. He read up on perspective and shading and how to measure distant objects using only a thumb and pencil. He got a sketch pad and blue 2H pencils and did some very passable drawings of women and chairs and sneakers before losing interest.

"Maybe draw a picture of the guy," said Keith. "We could make copies and hand them around a little bit."

"That's a good idea."

"You have some friends. Roland Miles would probably love anything to do with the possibility of violence. Does he know?"

"Yeah."

"And there's the police."

"I don't want to tell them," said Pierre. "The first thing they'd want to know is where the money is. And if you don't say anything about the money, there's nothing for them to act on. You know, 'There's this guy, maybe, I don't know his name or where he is.' Hell, they wouldn't even write it down."

"You know Telegram Sam?"

Nicknamed for his terse manner of speaking, Telegram Sam was a state trooper operating out of the Gamelon barracks who came into the Jack of Diamonds sometimes.

"I've seen him," said Pierre.

"You should tell him."

"I'll think about that. Did you ever have anybody after you?"

"One time, yeah," said Keith. "There was this friend of mine, and we were in a bar in La Crosse, and somebody was giving him a hard time about something. I don't remember what anymore. This was years ago. So anyway I told the guy to shut up, not my friend but this other guy. And he did. Backed right down, which was kind of a lesson to me, and I thought that was that. But then him and *his* friends found me a couple of weeks later in another bar and beat me up pretty good. You know. They'd come off from working in a factory and I was sort of drunk, so you can imagine how it went. That was the night I lost my hat. First hat I ever bought on my own. Got it at a men's store for, like, twenty-nine dollars."

Keith was silent for a moment, remembering his hat.

"So don't do what I did," he said. "I did nothing. That was a mistake."

That night Pierre went home and attempted to draw the driver of the pickup. He sat at his big steel desk with a goosenecked lamp and paper and pencil and Artgum eraser. He worked on the drawing for over an hour, sketching the figure as he remembered it behind the wheel of the pickup and half turned toward the viewer.

The face gave him trouble. Faces always had. Sometimes he would leave them blank, which looked more artistic than it sounded. Eyes were hard to get right. Too much detail, they looked crazy. Too little, they looked like coal. In this case, he tried to convey the Distinguished Expert's evasiveness by having his eyes look to one side. But it only seemed that something interesting was happening off the edge of the page.

He remembered what he had thought of the driver based on his face. That he was dishonest and felt sorry for himself and used this feeling to motivate and justify whatever he felt like doing. It was often self-pity that made people greedy and mean. But Pierre had little luck translating these impressions back to the physical characteristics that had made them. He drew and erased over and over. Artgum crumbs littered the paper and the desk.

Even at the height of his drawing powers he had not been able to draw faces.

It's an odd and disconcerting thing to imagine that someone is pursuing you without any evidence beyond the assumption that they probably would be.

You put yourself in the mind of the imagined chaser, try to guess what he is thinking. You almost end up pulling for him or offering helpful advice. *Why not call the bars? That's how I found the woman I sent all your cash to.*

Maybe he was a self-taught artist too, and had drawn a picture of Pierre, and now the two faced off over an unknown distance armed with their crude and unrecognizable sketches.

Pierre slept with a pipe wrench near the bed in case he had to get up and smack somebody with it. He listened for footsteps outside the door and, when he heard them, stepped out to make sure it was nothing, not bringing the wrench, because he knew he could never really hit anyone with it, and thus ending up in the worst position if it had been something, which it never was.

He wondered how it would end, imagined the different ways. On the shore. On a hill. On sand, grass, soft wooden boards. Or in a house, with threadbare carpet and a candle guttering on the sideboard.

The sun goes down and the wind gusts outside the door. There is a certain amount of standing around. Guns go off like sounds on TV. Someone dies and there they are, dead forever, hard to believe as it may be. Music plays, distant music.

Truly, he thought that nothing would come of it. For that is usually the case. People spend their lives imagining the worst and best things when more typically it's the middle thing that happens.

Probably because he had kept the money for less than a week, it did not seem that real to him. And as he had read somewhere, money is only a symbol of what it can buy. But $77,000 is a symbol of a lot of things that could be bought.

He wondered who first thought of money and

whether they didn't have a hard time getting people to take the idea seriously.

Pierre resented the time that thinking of these things required. He liked to start each moment fresh, not worrying about something from two months ago or even ten minutes ago. He wanted to keep his eyes to the front and be free of the past.

Nonetheless, he joined a self-defense class in Desmond City.

The instructor was a short and rather wizened man named Geoff Lollard who had a storefront by the railroad yards. Lollard was getting up there in years and his meager appearance was a selling point. He must be really good because he didn't look that good at all.

Lollard and Pierre sat on folding chairs and talked before Pierre's first class. The course was called Strike, Deflect, Marginalize, and the students did not wear white robes because Lollard thought they created a false sense of achievement, although, he said, he could have made a lot of money selling white robes over the years. He said that the martial arts movies had given people unrealistic expectations. You would not be able to fly or run across a lake or stand around in willow trees, as in *Crouching Tiger, Hidden Dragon.*

"But what a great movie," said Pierre.

"Perhaps," said Geoff Lollard. "But you don't know

what was great about it. When you've trained for one year, watch it again, and you will see the great parts."

"I like the ending."

"That isn't one of them."

"It really got to me."

"I suppose. I wasn't watching for emotion but for more technical aspects. Now, tell me, Mr. Hunter. You are in a fight. What's the goal?"

"To win."

"No."

"Well, then I don't know."

"Think of a fight as two floors of a building. The first floor is the beginning of the fight, the second floor the ending. There is an escalator and there is an elevator. Which do you want to take?"

"The escalator," said Pierre.

"And I prefer the elevator. Do you get that?"

"Not really."

"There is your way, and your opponent's way, and they're not the same. The fight is the process of finding out which way it's going to be. If you only think of winning, you're looking past what you need to see."

"You want them to play your game."

"Yes. That's what is meant by marginalizing. Now, I think we should do some sparring so I know where your skills are. Try to hit me in any way you're comfortable with."

"With a fist?"

"It doesn't matter."

Lollard wound an egg timer and they went around for ninety seconds. Pierre spent most of the time backing up and laughing, painful though the experience was. It embarrassed him to be battered around the mat by this strange little martial arts teacher. Finally Lollard jabbed a heel into Pierre's solar plexus and Pierre stood with his hands on his knees gasping for air.

"Did not see that coming," he said.

"The kick is one of the easiest things to deal with if you know what you're doing," said Lollard. "Maybe we'll begin with kicking."

Pierre worked out three times a week in the novice class through the month of September. There he reached a kind of peaceful exhaustion that he had not known since his football days in high school. Afterward he would go to a bench in the park where he had gone before his arrest on New Year's Eve and drink a bottle of Foster's. Face hot from the exercise, he would sit in the shadows of the afternoon.

One day the Carbon Family were setting up their instruments for a concert in the park. The lead singer, Allison Kennedy, came over and sat on the bench in a white crepe dress with red and black flowers.

"Hey, I heard you're seeing my cousin," she said.

"Stella," said Pierre.

"Yeah."

"She's your cousin? I didn't know that."

"What do you know about her?"

"What should I?"

"Just be careful. That's all I have to say."

"Why?"

"Well, now, she fell; you know that."

"No, I didn't. Fell from what?"

"A ladder. She was taking down storm windows and she fell off the ladder. The oil guy found her beside the house. It was pretty bad. She was in the hospital a long time. They didn't think she would even live."

"When was this?"

"I don't know. A year and a half ago, I guess. Not last spring but the spring before."

"She seems all right now."

"I hope that's true," said Allison, "but I wouldn't know. See, because, when she got out of the hospital, she was like another person. She didn't want anything to do with her family. I tried to go see her; she wouldn't come to the door. Instead, there was some old man there I'd never seen before. He said she wasn't taking visitors. I gave him some flowers, you know, that were for her."

"Was this here or in Wisconsin?"

"Here. At the lake. What about Wisconsin?"

"She's from there. She told me."

"No, she isn't. Stella always lived here. This is what

I mean, Pierre. Something went wrong in her mind; I'm sorry, it did. The doctors said they had no reason to keep her. But they would've had plenty of reason if they knew her."

"Maybe she wanted to forget what happened. And this was her way of doing it."

Allison Kennedy held out her hand and he put the Foster's in it and she took a drink and handed back the bottle.

"Look, you want to forget something, you forget it," she said. "You don't hide inside your house and tell people you're from Wisconsin."

Ned's rental-car business was in a square box of a building out on the edge of the airport. Jean was talking on the phone as Shane leaned on the counter and listened.

"A harmonica," she said. "Yeah. Very nice one. Silver with—um, inlays. I found it down beside the seat and I thought, Now, where did this come from? So that's when I remembered this guy I gave a ride to. But the problem is I didn't get what his name is. It might be Pete. Or it might be Pat. All I really know is he was catching rides back from California and lives somewhere around you. So I'm calling all over the place hoping to find him because I know he would want this harmonica back. It seems like a family heirloom maybe.... Yeah.... Okay."

She covered the mouthpiece with her hand. "They're checking," she said.

Shane picked up a red stapler and sprang back the top to see if there were staples in it. "What if he doesn't have a harmonica?"

"How would they know that? Maybe he just started playing."

"You should say it's a check, you found a check."

"Wouldn't that have his name on it?"

"Oh, right."

"Hello?" said Jean. "Yeah, hi.... You do? Really?... Uh-huh. California. The state.... Yes, that's possible. Well, does he hitchhike?... Sure. Anyone would. Okay, and what's the name again?... Great. He'll be so happy to get that harmonica back."

She hung up the phone and wrote something on a pad of paper.

"They know him?" said Shane. "Who is he?"

She tore the sheet from the pad and handed it to him. "Don't make too much of it. This could be him but I wouldn't bet on it. They said he goes to Wyoming to fish and maybe California, but they weren't sure."

"Who were you talking to?"

"A fireman in some place called Arcadia. And he said this guy might hitchhike, but probably only if his car broke down."

"Why a fireman?"

"Fire departments know everything in these little burgs."

"Hmm, I don't know," said Shane.

"It's the one lead I have so far," said Jean.

A stack of maps stood on the counter, and Shane took one and stapled it to the piece of paper. "Keep calling, okay?"

"I will."

Just then a man came into the office. He wore a blue suit coat and tan pants, and his hair was thin and combed into a crest above his head.

"I'm Mr. Bromley," he said. "I just got in from Milwaukee and I should have a Malibu reserved, I think."

Jean shuffled the papers on her desk. "Why, yes, Mr. Bromley, here you are. I'll need to see your driver's license and a credit card."

He took these from his billfold and handed them to her, and she looked thoughtfully from the license to the man and back to the license.

"Is something wrong?" he said.

"I'm sorry," said Jean. "I was just confused, because you look younger in person than in your photograph. I hope you don't mind."

"Of course not."

"You know, security and all."

"No, I understand that. I'm in the security business myself."

"Well, thank God someone is these days." She touched the links of her necklace. "The things you read, you don't even want to read them. By the way, we have a special today on the Park Avenue. I'm not trying to force it on you, but some people want to know, because the Park Ave's just a little *nicer*."

"But you have a Malibu on the lot."

"Oh, yes. It's back by the fence," said Jean. "Supposed to be very peppy."

"And how much more is the Park Avenue?"

"Twenty-nine dollars and change."

"I'll tell you what I'll do."

"What will you do, Mr. Bromley?"

After the customer departed in the Park Avenue, Jean said, "And that is how that's done."

"If that guy's in the security business, you can see why there's no security," said Shane. "I need a car."

"Take the Malibu."

Pierre and Stella were sitting on the sofa reading at her house one night toward the end of September. It was cool in the room and a table fan turned slowly on an old wooden crate because they liked the sound. Stella read the time book that he'd given her and Pierre read *Stories of Red Hanrahan*, which had been written by Yeats "with Lady Gregory's help."

After a while Stella put her book down. She

reached for the ceiling, tilted her head, and yawned. Her eyes widened, her hands curled into fists with the knuckles touching overhead, and she said, "Yow," in a high soft voice.

It was the most beautiful yawn Pierre had ever seen. She was wearing a sleeveless linen dress with an orange flower on the front. He'd been reading how Hanrahan lost a year's time after his meeting with the daughter of the Silver Hand.

"Was I ever here before, or where was I on a night like this?" said Hanrahan in the story.

"Where are you from in Wisconsin?" Pierre said.

"The northern part," she said. "Why?"

"I talked to somebody I know. Allison Kennedy."

"Oh, yes."

"She said she's your cousin and that you always lived here."

Stella got up and walked barefoot around the room. She made a steeple of her fingers and pressed them to her lips and then brushed the front of the linen dress.

"What else did she say?"

"Is she your cousin?"

"Yes."

"That you fell off a ladder and almost died, and after that you weren't the same."

"That's true too," said Stella. "And that of course is

what hurt them and why they tell stories about me. They said I had changed. And I had. I'm sorry this is painful. But I can't bring back that day. I can't bring back the person they knew."

"It's all right, Stella."

"But when they say I never lived in Wisconsin, I don't understand it. How would they know? Have they written down every place I ever was? Were they following me around with a notebook?"

"I doubt it," said Pierre.

"People change. They move from state to state. Is this really so hard to believe?"

"Look, I don't care where you're from. And I'm sorry you fell, but that doesn't change anything for me."

She took the book from his hands and put it with the other one on the wooden crate, and she lay on the sofa with her feet up on the back.

"Except I want to put up your storms this fall," said Pierre.

"Will you come here?" she said.

"Yeah."

"Will you please?"

Sometimes Shane dreamed about the woman who died in the fire. Once he was crossing a field beside a river and she followed him at ten paces and never said a word, except finally to ask where he was going, and he said San Antonio, and she said that's what she thought.

In another dream she appeared as an angel of revenge in a horse-drawn chariot coming down backlit by a full moon over a party in someone's yard. She was just a speck at first but grew to fill up the moon. The happiness of the crowd at seeing an angel turned to pure running fear as she began firing tridents upon them from a longbow.

Strangely enough, Shane liked the second dream better. He preferred to imagine space as the home of superhuman warriors rather than an endless emptiness with broken rocks spinning through on their way to nowhere. Even if the warriors were coming for him.

Yes, he thought. It is how they said.

He'd grown up in an honest family in the city of Limonite near the Canadian border. Two brothers, three sisters. His father managed a hatchery and his mother was a paralegal. Shane started stealing electronic equipment in college and had saved $19,000 by the time he got a bachelor's degree in communication. After graduation he went in for housebreaks. He learned about silver and gold and porcelain and furniture and began to know what was worth having and what wasn't. Sometimes he would drive down to Chartrand, where the money was good, and that's how he met Ned, who then had an antiques store along with his other businesses.

*　*　*

The house fire was simple on paper and to do. It was a vacation house in the town of St. Ivo, Wisconsin, and the owner wanted it destroyed so his wife would not get it in a divorce settlement. He said the house had been empty for months and his wife was on a cruise to Alaska so she wouldn't be there. It seemed like a pretty bitter enterprise, but as Ned said, you see everything at one time or another. He gave Shane a map and an address and a picture of the house, and Shane drove the three and a half hours to St. Ivo and found the house in late afternoon. It was an old place out in the country with silver shingles and trellises and dormers all around.

Then Shane went east another hour and got a motel room and returned to St. Ivo in the middle of the night. He broke a basement window and pried off the lock plate and opened the window and climbed inside. He shone a flashlight around the basement, found an old stuffed chair, pulled it over by the stairs, and jammed newspapers down in it. Then he laid some wine bottles around for misleading evidence and started the newspapers on fire and left the house. He stood in the treeline long enough to see the fire coming up in the windows, and then he drove back to the motel.

Ned called Shane in Limonite some days later and told him that a house sitter had been hired by the wife.

She had been a ski instructor and had died in a bedroom on the third floor.

Shane's criminal career tailed off beginning then. He felt cheated by the death on his hands. He became random and blunt where once he'd been deft and professional. He started breaking into cars again, and sometimes he would only cut up the seats and kick the dashboard apart without taking anything.

His good money was gone in little over a year. He lost a car to the bank and his landlord took him to court to have him evicted. But then a security guard he knew told him a story. It seemed that the manager of a car wash in Limonite had been skimming from the receipts for years and putting the money in a safe inside his house. The guard speculated that he and Shane might break into the house and open the safe with a cutting torch.

Shane talked him out of it. Too risky, he said, and the money would probably burn in the process. The guard did not read between the lines of Shane's refusal. Had he been aware enough to do so, he probably would not have mentioned the safe to Shane anyway. The guard didn't want to do the job, he only wanted to dream about doing the job.

But a few nights later, Shane went in his old blue pickup to the house of the manager of the car wash and got him to open the safe. It took about half an hour of yelling and knocking him around. He was a thin man in his forties with a large collection of sports memorabilia and stubborn with the years of squirreling the money away and knowing it would always be there. Shane tied the man to a radiator before he left, but he didn't tie him very well, it turned out, because as Shane was driving away the man came out of the house with a rifle and shot a hole in the window of Shane's truck.

At first you could hardly see where the bullet had gone through the glass but overnight the window cracked into a thousand pieces and Shane pushed them out into the pickup bed and swept them onto the ground.

"Did you hear about Pete?" said Roland Miles.

"Pete who?"

Pierre and Roland were walking north out of Shale in the right-of-way beside the railroad tracks. They had their rifles and were going to a grove a mile out where they would shoot at bottles.

"Oh, you know. *Pete*. What the hell's his name."

Pierre studied some jet contrails that had fanned out against the light blue arc of the sky. "Pete at the hardware store?"

"No," said Roland. "He's always at the Clay Pipe Inn. Sells, I don't know, cleaning products door-to-door or some shit. It's like one of those jobs you can't figure out how he got it or how he makes any money."

"Pete Marker."

"Yeah. Why couldn't I think of that."

"Why, what'd he do?"

"He got robbed."

"I didn't hear that."

"Well, he's leaving the Laundromat in Arcadia the other night, getting in his car, you know, and it's just like in the movies, 'cause there's some guy *in* the car already, down in the backseat, with a knife."

"I thought Pete Marker drove a pickup."

"Yeah, but extended cab."

"So what'd he want?"

"Money. Had some big folding knife. And, of course, Pete Marker, you know, he's got like four dollars on him or something. Guy never has any fucking money. He owes more money than you could possibly steal off him."

"He must have been scared."

"Hell, yes, he was. He went back in the Laundromat all shaking. They didn't believe him at first. They're, like, 'Calm down, Pete.'"

"And where did the knife guy go?"

"Got away."

"Strange," said Pierre.

"Isn't it? When's the last time somebody got stuck up with a knife in Arcadia?"

"I don't know."

"For four dollars? That's right, because it never happens. So I was thinking. Pete Marker. Pierre Hunter.

Some Pierres are actually *called* Pete. This might be the guy you took the money from."

"That would make more sense if he knew my name."

"I know, you said that. But you ride all the way from Minnesota and never once, 'Hi, I'm So-and-so?' It doesn't make sense."

"Well, you don't hitchhike. It's not like the Chamber of Commerce."

"Somebody stops, you know, 'Here, get in. What's your name, stranger?' and you're like, 'Fuck off'? I don't get it."

"Oh, I might have told him," said Pierre. "I don't care if I did. I've been working out at the Geoff Lollard school."

"I hope you know what a joke that sounds like."

"I do. That's why I said it. But it is a good workout."

"What if he has a knife?"

"There is a way to get a knife. You take hold of the hand it's in and smash it against something until they let go of it."

"And you can do this?"

"Well, I don't know, but this is the first I've heard of a knife."

They walked along with the sound of their boots on the gravel beside the railroad ties.

"I laugh in the face of danger," said Pierre.

"You do."

"Yeah. You should hear me."

Roland raised his hand as if taking an oath. "What's that?"

Pierre stopped and listened. Something was moving away from them in the grass between the tracks and the fence. Roland saw the animal first and then Pierre did too as it ran along the fencerow with its champagne coat shining in the sun.

"What is that?" said Pierre.

"I would say that is a badger," said Roland.

Stella sat at the edge of land beyond the trees, and the lake lay below her with the moon's reflection riding on the water. Tim Geer knelt nearby, idly flipping a knife off the back of his hand so that it turned over once in the air and landed point down in the dirt.

"How much longer will it be?" she said.

"Soon," he said. "Have patience. I have one more bit to do, but your part is done. In fact it's more than done."

"What do you mean?"

"You're too close to Hunter, that's what I mean."

"I want to tell him everything."

"He won't believe it if you do."

"I just feel like we set him up."

"Set him up? You pulled him from that water, where he was going to die."

"But for what? I'm saying. To die another way."

"I don't know that he will."

"Yeah, you do."

"He took the money. I didn't make him do that."

"You knew he would."

Tim took the knife from the dirt and wiped the blade by drawing it between the thumb and finger of his left hand.

"Two different things," he said.

"You said you have something left to do," she said. "What is it?"

"I have to get lost."

"How do you mean?"

"I better not say."

They got up and walked back through the evergreens toward the light of Stella's house. At the edge of the clearing the pale form of a barn owl flopped in the grass and lay still and flopped again. Stella picked up the owl with her hands around its wings and looked into its dark and divided eyes. Then she raised her hands and opened them and the owl flew up and on its way.

Tim drove off and Stella went into the house and up to bed. She lay in the dark thinking for a long time.

Tim had a point. Pierre would not believe what had happened to her. No one would.

She had wakened in a burning room, with the walls breaking open in flames, and she had made for the window. But the fire moved the same way, washing over her and pushing her to the floor, and only when she emerged from the window and did not fall did she understand that she had gone between lives. She had done this before, she knew what it was, but never from violence.

For weeks she traveled the countryside with no more form than a shadow. She was looking for Tim Geer. He was not easy to find, because very few could hear her when she spoke, and even fewer were brave enough to answer.

Yet those who did answer tended to know Tim, or they had heard of him, or they knew of someone who had met him, and day by day she made her way toward the Driftless Area, where late one afternoon she found him in his backyard on the outskirts of Eden Center, tending a trash fire with a stick.

"Can you help me?" she said.

He looked around. "I'll try."

"You hear what I say."

"Clearly."

"I'm in kind of a predicament."

"You've died," he said. "There was a fire."

"That's right," she said. "And I have to find the one who started it."

"Maybe it was electrical."

"I don't think so."

"I would know more if I could take your hand. But for that you would need hands."

"Yes, that's the other thing."

"You come back tomorrow," he said.

She returned the next afternoon at the same time. Tim was walking around the kitchen of his house sorting returnable bottles and cans and putting them in wicker baskets.

"I talked to a nurse I know," he said. "Asked for hopeless cases to pray for. So she names this person and that one. Mostly old, like me. Then she says they got this young lady Stella Rosmarin in the hospital down in Desmond City. Awful story, really. She fell off a ladder and hit her head. They've had her on a machine of some kind for two months."

"She won't get better?"

"Doesn't sound that way. And if she will, you'll know."

"Can you take me there?"

"Sure," said Tim.

They rode to Desmond City in Tim's car, an old beige Nova with woven seat covers. The receptionist at the hospital said Stella Rosmarin was in Five South and no one but family could see her.

She said goodbye to Tim and went up to the ICU and found Stella in a silver bed where her life was being carried on by mechanical means. The transfer was unstoppable, once she was near, like gravity, like the completion of the fall she might have made from the window of the burning house. She lay quietly for a while, feeling the robotic rhythm of the machine and the sadness of two deaths.

Then she wrenched her hands from the rails where they'd been bound by light blue tape. She pulled off the mask of the respirator and sat up, drawing air into her lungs. A man in sea-green hospital clothes came and stood looking at her, saying nothing.

"It's all right," she said. "I don't need these things."

Then more doctors came. They passed a clipboard around and stared at the clipboard and at the red numbers on the monitors and at her.

"Where are you?" said one.

"In a hospital."

"How did you get here?"

"I came up the stairs."

"What's your name?"

"Stella."

SEVEN

Stella's bicycle leaned on its kickstand by the door of the Jack of Diamonds. She was standing in the kitchen with Keith Lyon, who was introducing himself by showing her how he chopped onions.

With a red-handled knife from Sweden he made a series of incisions until the onion was crosshatched like a globe but still in one piece and then with a sweep of the blade he spilled an array of perfectly diced pieces onto the cutting board.

"I don't believe that," said Stella.

"I'll do another one," said Keith. "Watch closely this time."

"I was watching closely."

"Hey, Keith," said Pierre. He stood in the doorway. "The state cop's out here. Telegram Sam."

"For what?" said Keith.

"I don't know."

Pierre, Keith, Stella, and Charlotte Blonde gathered in the bar. The state trooper stood before them in tall black boots and with his hands resting on his utility belt.

"Looking for a man," he said. "Timothy Geer of Eden Center. Seventy-four years old. Last seen yesterday afternoon at Small Art Cinema. Arrived forty minutes early for the matinee. Informed ticket taker he would take walk in woods before movie. Headed down road in this direction. Presumably took one of the trails between here and there. Never came back, near as we know. His car still at movie house. Subject is five ten, hundred and eighty pounds, wearing black-and-green plaid coat. Anyone seen him?"

They shook their heads. The name meant something only to Stella, but she said nothing.

"All right. By the theater's count this man's been in the woods twenty-five hours. Search dogs on way but not here yet. Two hours' light left. Need volunteers. Pairs to walk the trails. Very simple. Go out, come back."

The Jack of Diamonds did not open until five-thirty, so they agreed to lock up and go. Telegram Sam led them out to the parking lot, where he divided them into two teams and gave each a trail map and a radio from the trunk of his cruiser.

"Preset channels," he said. "All link to me. Stay in touch. Push is talk, let up is listen. No need to touch nothing else. One map, one radio, one team. Buddy system. Do not lose sight of partner. Do not stray from trail. One lost; don't need more. Make noise. Call out. If you hear barking that means dogs have arrived. Nothing to fear."

"What kind of shoes is he wearing?" said Charlotte.

"No idea. Immaterial. Look for man, not at ground."

Pierre and Charlotte Blonde were one team. They went up the green trail for half an hour, arriving at the lookout tower where Roland Miles patched the mortar. The cold and rusted stairway took them to the light at the top. They stood looking out at the hills and ragged crowns of the evergreens.

"This radio is heavy," said Charlotte. "I bet it cost a thousand dollars. Here. Give him a call."

"Should I?"

"Yeah. He said to."

"What's his name?"

"Sam."

"That's not his real name, Charlotte. People call him Telegram Sam as a joke."

"Just say trooper."

"Good idea, buddy." Pierre pushed the button. "Trooper, this is Pierre Hunter on the green trail."

"Go ahead, Pierre."

"It's pretty windy. We haven't seen him. We're up in the tower."

"Copy, Pierre. Dogs here."

"What?"

"Dogs in woods."

"Ten four," said Pierre.

"Search dogs."

Pierre put the radio in his coat pocket.

"Ten four?" said Charlotte. "You ass."

Keith and Stella crossed the ridge a mile northeast of the tavern and the path started down. They walked along calling for Tim Geer. The forest grew dark and there was a sound high in the trees.

"Do you hear that?"

"It's just the wind."

"They've got the dogs."

"Really," said Keith. "Guy's probably sitting home by the TV."

"No. He's here somewhere."

"Do you know him?"

"Kind of. He helped me out when I was new in town. The last time I saw him he told me he was going to get lost."

"That's a strange thing to say."

"I didn't know what he meant. But now I guess I do."

"Who would get themself lost on purpose?"

"Maybe he thought it would lead to something else."

"Like what?"

They came to a big tree that had fallen across the trail and they sat on the bark and swung their legs across. It was getting dark but back in the woods the white rocks held the light.

"That I couldn't tell you," said Stella.

When Charlotte Blonde was nervous she would talk about her baby—what she had learned to do or say, what she had figured out how to knock over, things like that.

They were far beyond the tower now, in a ravine, and the deep wet ground gave beneath their feet, and the wooded slopes rose left and right.

"Her latest deal is she wants to know how everything works," said Charlotte. "Like the other day she drags a suitcase from the closet and says, 'How works, Mom? How works?'"

"Wow, that's cute as hell," said Pierre.

"Yeah. You know, so I open the suitcase, put some clothes in it, whatever, then I say, 'This is for when you go away.'"

"So she understood."

"Well, no. Not at all. She somehow thought that I was going to send her away. So I said, 'Oh, no, honey. Not you without me. But if *we* went away. On a trip.'"

"She seems kind of jumpy."

"Well, she is. Where are we?"

"I don't know," said Pierre. "There should be paint on the trees."

"I'm not seeing paint," said Charlotte.

The trail was gone. They looked at the map and because they didn't know where they were it was not helpful. But it seemed that if they went up the side of the ravine they might find the trail and even if they didn't they would be moving into daylight, which seemed advisable. So they climbed the north slope by leaning parallel to it and pulling themselves along by the trunks of trees.

After about twenty minutes Pierre and Charlotte reached the top of the ravine and came out onto a high field with long grass and rows of trees snarled with vines and runners. The sun was going down behind hills that were miles away.

"It's an orchard," said Pierre.

"I see that."

They walked at a right angle to the tree rows, looking up and down and seeing only birds darting across the open spaces. It was quiet and strange in the orchard but they were relieved to be in a place where people had once worked. In a little while they came up behind a silvery shed maybe twelve by fifteen, and walking around to the front they found an abandoned road on the other side.

An unroofed plank floor lay before the shed and Pierre stepped up onto the soft wooden boards and opened a paneled door and looked inside.

"This must be where they sold the apples," he said.

"Let's get out of here," said Charlotte. "We were asked to look; we looked. We did our part for society."

Pierre stepped into the shed. It was empty but for a wooden table with a drawer and some old bamboo rakes in a corner. Rafters ran crosswise beneath the peaked roof. He opened the drawer, which was divided into slots by intersecting wooden lath.

"Come on, Pierre," said Charlotte, from the doorway. "I don't even want to be here, let alone traipse around in some godforsaken building."

Then a voice called out Pierre's name and he jumped in the darkness of the shed, but it was only the radio in the pocket of his coat.

"Man found," said Telegram Sam. "All is well. Come back. Subject in good shape."

Charlotte took the radio from Pierre's coat, pressed the button, and said, "Who found him?"

"The dogs."

They walked down the abandoned road, a green tunnel through the trees, reasoning that it must go down to the highway. Prairie grass and maple saplings filled the roadbed. After a quarter mile Pierre ran into a chain hidden in the grass and fell over it. He got up and lifted the chain and saw that it ran across the road anchored to trees on either side.

"They ought to give you some warning on that," said Charlotte.

Their long walk had taken Pierre and Charlotte Blonde up and around the Jack of Diamonds and when they came to the highway they were on a bend of the road south of the tavern and knew where they were and walked up around the bend to the parking lot.

There a pack of tricolor beagles strained at their leashes and bayed at the old man, Tim Geer, who sat eating a grilled cheese sandwich in the back of one of three police cruisers now in the lot. The dogs did not seem to realize that their job was done or maybe they only wanted the sandwich.

Pierre crossed the parking lot and stopped and put his hand on Charlotte's shoulder.

"I know that guy," he said. "He was in the park in Desmond City on New Year's Eve."

"Talk to him," said Charlotte. "All he's been through, he could probably stand seeing someone he knows."

Pierre walked over to the police car. The old man was sitting sideways on the seat with his feet on the ground and a Jack of Diamonds plate on his lap.

"Do you remember me?" said Pierre.

Tim Geer looked up with his calm and buried eyes. "Oh, yes."

"I got in trouble that night."

"You told me you knew what you were doing."

"I might have been exaggerating. So where were you?"

"All over the place. Once I got off the trail I sort of lost track of time. Spent the night in a little house."

"In an orchard."

"That's the one."

"You should have gone down the road that runs by it. It comes out eventually."

"Then you wouldn't have found it, would you?"

"The road or the house?"

"Either one."

"What difference does it make?"

"Think what you could do with a place like that."

"Start an orchard, I guess."

"I'm telling you as plain as I can. And I know it ain't that plain. But you have to think about it. What you could do."

"Hunter."

Pierre turned. Telegram Sam was waving him away from the patrol car.

"Mr. Geer's exhausted," he said. "Come with me."

* * *

They went around the Jack of Diamonds and sat down at the cable spools in back.

The state trooper lit a Chesterfield and flipped open a notebook. "Gee, it's great when things work out," he said. "Ain't it? I mean, we *practice* shit that doesn't go this well."

"Yeah," said Pierre. He had never heard Telegram Sam speak in sentences before.

"I'm thinking maybe you can help me, Pierre. I'm thinking of this knife incident over to Arcadia and maybe you might know something."

"What I heard, that's about it," said Pierre.

"All right, I'll tell you what I've found out and we can speak together in candor, I hope. On August the eighteenth you were riding in a pickup truck that ran off the interstate at the intersection of Highway 233. You were hitchhiking on the interstate, which is illegal, but I don't care about that at this time. The driver of the truck stole your suitcase but was rendered unconscious and so you got your suitcase back and went along your way. Am I right so far?"

"Who've you been talking to?"

"Never mind that. I'm right or I'm not."

"You are," said Pierre. "A backpack, but yeah."

"Now, the truck was registered to a Shane Hall, comes from up north, and, as near as we can tell, Hall was in fact the driver. Later that evening, which you may not be aware, Hall, or the man we believe to be Hall, stole a car driven by a woman who had stopped to determine whether the truck in the ditch needed towing. Now the stolen car later shows up in the Quad Cities in an accident, and it would appear that it had passed through several hands by that time, and we're working on that part of it. Or I'm not, but someone is. But the important thing about the car is that this Hall may be around here somewhere and operating under the alias of Bob Johnson or Bob Roberts. And that therefore he could be the guy with the hunting knife that went after Pete Marker, perhaps thinking he was you."

Pierre stretched his legs under the picnic table. "Well, yeah, *maybe*," he said. "I don't know how much of it's true."

"Nor do I. And normally we would say, two guys fighting over a backpack, you know, who gives a damn. But we have business with Hall if we can find him. The cops in Minnesota say he tied some guy to a radiator and put him in the hospital a couple days before you met him. So this, then, is my question to you. What was in that backpack?"

"Nothing. Clothes. He didn't know what was in it. It was just something he could steal."

"Did you take something else from this guy?"

"Did I take something?"

"Because the way I see it, when you put it all together it doesn't make sense. That he would be chasing you, okay. But."

"I never said he was chasing me."

"Well, there are those who think he might be. But why? That's the part I don't understand."

"I did knock him out."

"And how'd you do that?"

"Threw a rock."

"Into a moving truck. That's pretty good."

"Who told you it was moving?"

"Was it?"

"It was stopped."

"Okay, Pierre. Some people decide to do something if it makes sense or not and nothing's going to stop them. That does happen. But if you know more than you're telling me this is your chance to say so."

"I took the backpack and what was in it," said Pierre.

Pierre left work early that night and went to the Ship's Harbor in Desmond City.

This was a downtown bar with a maritime theme. A ship's prow and cabin projected diagonally from the corner of the building, and you could sit inside the ship on a raised platform and look out the windows. But Pierre sat at the four-sided bar next to a kid named Kevin Little who had been two years behind him in high school.

"Hey," said Pierre, and called him Little Kevin.

"Cut it out, I hate that," he said.

"It was your nickname."

"I always hated it."

"You should have said something."

"You were upperclassmen."

"Larger than life," Pierre suggested.

"It seemed that way."

"Really."

"Kind of, yeah."

"Miles might have been larger than life, but now he's just life-size. I was more of a loser."

"You are a loser."

"Probably so. But a beautiful woman loves me. So there is that."

"Why aren't you working?"

"We found a guy in the woods today."

"Dead?"

"No. He was lost. They brought in dogs. He'd been in there overnight."

"That's lucky."

"It wasn't ever going to happen any other way."

"What do you mean?"

"Take a coin. No, forget that. Take two coins. Put them on the bar. One heads, one tails. On the bar."

Little Kevin leaned sideways on the bar stool and dug into his pocket and put two quarters between his drink and Pierre's.

"Good," said Pierre. "Now, think of something that you wonder if it will happen or not. Okay? Are you thinking of it?"

"Yeah. My disability claim."

"What's your disability?"

"A metal press fell on my arm at work."

"You don't seem disabled."

"No, I am. Trust me. For certain things I have to do I'm pretty disabled."

"Well, that's rough. What else is new?"

"You were doing something with these coins."

"Oh, right. You want to know about your disability. Let heads stand for yes and tails for no. Now ask yourself, can they both be true?"

"What do you mean?"

"Can both coins? In other words, can you both get and not get the disability on your arm?"

"Well, no, of course not."

"So what you're telling me is one of these coins is accurate and the other one's a big liar. Even though the answer is in the future. And how could that be? Because the future has already happened."

"No, it hasn't."

"The coins say different."

Kevin picked up one of the coins and stared at it. "Nah, I don't buy that," he said.

"I just thought of it."

"It doesn't tell you anything if you think about it for very long."

"If all the events from the beginning of the world to the end were laid down from the start, I wouldn't call that nothing. And we just travel across them. Think of it."

"I'm thinking."

"Maybe the future's like someplace you've never been. Like Sydney, Australia. You ever been there?"

"I never have."

"Exactly," said Pierre. "Me neither." But we wouldn't say it hasn't happened yet just because we haven't been there. We wouldn't say it might be a big city or it might be a dump by the side of the road, and it won't be either one till we arrive."

"That's true. But if things have happened and nobody knows what they are, what difference does it make? It amounts to the same thing as if they haven't happened."

"I didn't say nobody knows. Maybe you and me don't. But if we knew how to see it.... if we remembered how.... maybe we could."

"Fortune-tellers."

"Real ones, though."

"You believe in that?"

"I'm beginning to wonder."

Kevin Little left and then came back after an hour or so. Pierre sat drinking gin and was pretty well drunk by now. Whenever things were changing he was wide open to inebriation.

"Where've you been, Kev?" he said.

"I went to get these," said Kevin Little. He showed Pierre his shoes, which were made of orange leather with brass buckles. "Guy I know bought them but they were too small."

"Interesting."

"I know."

"I've been thinking," said Pierre. "Forget what I said before."

"About what?"

"The coins. All that. I was just talking through my hat."

"Too bad I already wrote it all down while it was fresh in my mind."

Pierre laughed. "That's pretty good, Kevin."

Half an hour later Pierre looked up to see that it was midnight and the bar was empty but for three guys playing cutthroat at the pool table. He picked up his drink and went over to the ship part of the bar and sat on a bench at the long table looking out at the cars going by in the street. He wished his friends would show up with white boxes of food tied with strings and they could have a party. Charlotte, Keith, Stella, Roland Miles, Carrie, and even his mother and father, since it was only imagination. Monster could nose around for dropped food. Pierre could see the wine and candles and hear the laughter around the table. He would talk into Stella's ear. His parents would be proud to see them together.

"You could do something like that," he said.

The bartender came over and collected Pierre's empty glass. "Hey, Hunter, I hate to do this, but no more for you."

"No, that's okay," said Pierre. "My God, I understand. I of all people."

"Oh, and I forgot to tell you. You're getting your harmonica back."

Pierre wondered if harmonica was the latest word for mojo or karma. "What are you talking about?" he said.

"Some woman found it in her car."

"I don't have a harmonica."

He got up and headed for the door. He had to concentrate on walking in all its aspects, it's really quite complicated when you have to think about it, and halfway across the bar he stopped and put his hand flat to the pool table for balance.

But in so doing he messed up the lay of the table and the cutthroat players objected and a fairly incoherent argument followed. They had bet on the game and so they wanted Pierre to pay them ten dollars for throwing

161

it off, but since there were three of them, he could not understand how they had arrived at ten. Finally they told him to leave, and he said he would, as that's what he'd been trying to do anyway.

Pierre walked out to the MGA and put the top down. He felt all right to drive. The lights and houses of Desmond City fell away and the road curved on into the darkness between land and sky. The air was cold yet his face was hot and sweaty. Halfway home he pulled over and walked down beside the road and was sick in the ditch. Then he stood up and looked up and down the blacktop, feeling empty of all gin and confusion.

The next morning Pierre woke early to the happy and undeserved news that he had not a trace of hangover. And he thought it was true what they said about clear liquors.

He made coffee with sugar and fried some hash browns and put milk in the coffee and ketchup on the hash browns and sat in the kitchen eating and reading the *Register* and listening to the Old 97s on the CD player.

When he washed the dishes he sang along with the song about being born in the backseat of a Mustang on a cold night in a hard rain. Then he took his shotgun and the thin aluminum case that held the cleaning kit from the broom closet and set them out on the table.

At midday he went down to the alley and took the MGA out into the streets of Shale. They were getting ready for Bank Robbery Days weekend, with banners across the street. This was an annual event celebrating Shale's sole bit of historical fame, a failed heist of 1933 about which songs had been written and a book as well.

The robbers were three brothers who set out to copy the Dillinger raids but had no luck at it. One left a coat with his name written inside the collar in the bank. Another gave their own getaway car a flat tire by throwing nails on the pavement to hinder pursuit. Finally, late in the day, the brothers found refuge by taking over a farmhouse with a family in it.

The high point of the weekend was a play staged in a machine shed on the site of the original farm. Entitled *Hostages to Fortune*, it told how the robber brothers broke in on the family and during a long tense evening came to understand that their situation was not too promising.

Pierre had seen the play many times. It was funny even when it wasn't trying to be. The big scene was a chess game played between the youngest robber and the father of the family, whose fear of the intruders has by this time turned more to scornful exasperation.

Pierre ended up at the golf course where Carrie Miles was in her office writing names on a chalkboard. Roland's graduation picture hung on the wall.

He looked wary in the photograph, as if listening to a complicated offer that might be a ripoff.

"Hey, you," said Carrie.

"Let's go for a ride."

"Where to?"

"Nowhere special."

"Let me finish these, then I will," she said. "Our last big weekend is coming up. You can read my poem while you wait. It's the longest one I've ever done."

She said she had entered the poem in the Bank Robbery Days poetry contest. It was called "Lust for Larceny," and this is how it began:

> *The hapless brothers fell upon the town*
> *Set on taking the People's Bank down.*
> *But every wild dream that you've ever seen*
> *Was sheer eloquence compared to their scheme.*
> *Incapable from start to finish, they*
> *Barreled ahead with the vault robbery,*
> *Ignoring somehow the mezzanine guard,*
> *Who, coming down behind the banister,*
> *Managed to fire a tear gas canister....*

Carrie's poem ran on for many lines and three pages. It described the robbery and getaway and ended in a bit of a twist by questioning the town's obsession with bank robberies.

For I wonder if we are not lame
To glory in faded criminal fame.
Or, on the other hand, it just might be
That we retain a lust for larceny
Born in the old times of prehistory,
When what you lost was better for me.

Her chalk made a soft insistent sound on the board as Pierre finished the poem.

"This is epic, Carrie," he said. "I mean it. I've never seen anything like it."

"Yeah, thanks. I read up on it," she said. "Of course I know it will never win. It challenges too many assumptions."

"It ought to win. But I think the way that prize works is old ladies giving it to other old ladies."

They rode out in the MGA, which Carrie had not seen since Pierre got it back. They passed the old Hunter house and went up to the power plant and parked by the fence as they had seven years before.

"How strange this seems," said Carrie. "Why were we here? Was it Skip Day? I remember being here, but why?"

"Rebecca Lee sent you to break up with me."

She turned sideways in the seat with an excited grin. "Oh God, that's right. I was so mean to you! I remember now."

"That wasn't mean," said Pierre. "I didn't really even care that much. I thought it was kind of nice that you wanted to go for a drive."

"We were all mean. It was in our nature. We didn't know what we were doing."

"I saw Kevin Little last night. Turns out he hated being called Little Kevin."

"Wouldn't you?" said Carrie.

"Yes, I would."

"This car is like a time machine. You can forget everything that's happened."

"How's Roland?"

"He's going on a canoe trip to the Boundary Waters. We can't use the dining room table because it's covered with pemmican and ripstop nylon."

"He'll miss the show."

"Oh, you know him; he hates it anyway. Says it's fakey and crowded. He's so moody. One of these times he'll go and not come back."

"Maybe that's what you want, you say it so much."

"Well, it is, sometimes. But I think I would be lonely if it happened. It's just that I thought life was going to be fun. That was really the impression that I had."

"It is fun," said Pierre. "Don't you think? I mean it's not like Adventureland. But you write your poems, the leaves move, you get laid sometimes. Isn't that fun?"

"The leaves move?"

"You know what I mean."

"Oh, joy, the leaves are moving."

"Honest to Christ, I believe that."

"I know you do."

Then Pierre heard a muffled sound and Carrie took a silver cell phone from her purse and checked the number on the screen and shut off the phone.

"Let me see that," said Pierre.

She handed it to him.

"Very modern," he said.

A train of five lime-green barges was going through the lock on the river, a deliberate process yet impressive in the way of all things that move slowly but with great mass.

The barges were long and sealed and immaculate, and a man stood on one of them with his foot up on a hatch and his arm resting on his knee.

Pierre and Stella sat on a bench on the observation platform watching the bargeman's incremental approach.

"What do you have on there?" Pierre called.

"Gypsum," he said.

"Hard to believe there's call for all that gypsum in the world," Pierre said to Stella.

"I don't know how much call there is for gypsum," she said.

"I think they use it in cement."

"Pierre."

"What?"

"I want you to go away for a while."

"Yeah?"

She slid down with her legs straight before her and her head resting on the back of the bench. "Go back to California. Go anywhere. For a week. Then it'll be done."

"What will?"

"How did you put it? *The hour is upon us.* It is. They're coming for the money."

"They."

"The one you got it from and two others."

"How do you know?"

"I just do. I have since the winter."

Pierre looked at the man on the green barge. He was about twenty feet farther down than he was before, and beyond the barges the iron-green river turned in deep and beveled circles.

"The winter," said Pierre. "Stella, I'd never even met the guy in the winter."

"I knew you would fall through the ice," she said. "I knew that you would find the one with the money and bring him here."

"I kind of put that together. You said have weapons. You said get ready. And I got ready."

"I don't think so, Pierre. I don't think you were ever going to be. This guy is badder than you think."

"You've been after him awhile, I take it."

"Yeah."

"What'd he do?"

"He burned down a house in Wisconsin. Killed the house sitter. And walked away from it."

"What's supposed to happen to him?"

"He dies. But it doesn't have to be you that does it. I think he'll bring it on himself some other way."

"Who was the house sitter?"

"Does it matter?"

"It must."

"You won't believe it."

"Hell, I think I already know."

Pierre got up and walked to the edge of the platform and stood with his back against the railing.

"You were the house sitter," he said.

She picked up a book of matches and tore a match out and tossed it on the concrete. "Not as I am now," she said. "I came here after the fire. You couldn't have seen me then. I was only the spirit of the life I had lived. Do you see what I mean?"

"You weren't Stella."

"No, I became her. She was gone, Pierre. She was only on a machine in the hospital."

"You know, I dreamed about you and a room with fire in it."

"You have some of that in you."

"Whose side is Tim Geer on?"

"Mine. And yours too, in a way. He makes things happen. So they go one way instead of the other."

"How?"

"I don't know. I'm not even sure he knows. I'm sorry, Pierre."

"Don't be," he said. "You saved my life. I haven't forgot that. And I won't let you down if I can figure out how not to."

EIGHT

THE MEN swung the red cones of flashlights as the cars bumped over the pasture of the farm and the headlights rose and fell.

The play about the bank robbers' occupation of the farmhouse in 1933 would soon begin. The machine shed stood ready with lights and bleachers and a stage version of the interior of the old house.

Pierre parked and walked across the field. Clouds rolled across the sky, rimmed silver by the hidden moon. The shed was a large corrugated steel building with flat roof and sloping sides. The sliding doors stood open, revealing the lights and people inside.

He felt odd echoes of the excitement of going to parties as a teenager. He had always expected to find something brilliant and wonderful. Instead he would become drunk and foolish, pass out, burn his hand with a cigarette. Young as he was, he had wasted a lot of time.

People milled around a bar table set up near the front of the machine shed. Pierre looked around to see who was there. Minburn the teacher had brought his history students. State Rep Denise Blasco handed out small American flags. Carrie Miles stood alone in a lavender dress and white sweater.

"Don't you look nice," said Pierre.

"Well, we try, and that's all we can do," she said. "Where's the little miss? Stella for star?"

"I don't know."

"Oh. My poem didn't win either, if it's any consolation."

"Too honest, probably."

"Maybe. I never heard a word about it."

"Would you like a drink?"

"Yes, I think so."

Pierre got them hard cider in paper cups, and as the lights went down they walked up beside the bleachers and found a place to sit on hay bales along the wall. Knowing well how the play began they looked not at the stage but at the open doors and the darkness beyond them.

In a little while a car pulled up and parked on the gravel outside. It was a round-fendered vintage sedan and moving very slowly, as according to the legend it was supposed to have a flat tire.

The three actors playing the robber brothers got out of the car and walked into the shed carrying shotguns under their arms. The doors rolled shut behind them to create an ominous feel and also to conserve heat. The bleachers slanted down in two banks, making three aisles, and each actor took a separate way to the stage.

Meanwhile, the man and woman playing the farm couple stepped onto the set and moved to their places in the kitchen.

The brothers gathered at the center of the stage and one of them made a knocking motion as if on a door, though there was none. The sound-effects man produced three sharp raps, whose imperfect coordination with the gesture was considered part of the fun.

The woman looked up from the newspaper she was reading at the kitchen table.

"I wonder who that could be," she said.

"This hour of night," said the man.

"Open the door quickly. They'll wake the children with that knocking."

"I'll open the door."

"Hey, good idea," said Pierre.

The woman folded her paper and pushed her hair back. "Actually, I wouldn't mind having visitors. It does get awfully quiet out here."

"We have card parties."

"I wish there were more card parties."

"Farming's no easy life, I know that," said the man.

"We get up in darkness and lay down in darkness, and many's the time we don't have much to show for it."

"I always thought there should be a song here," said Carrie.

"I know," said Pierre.

Again came the knocking of the brothers.

"Someone is still at the door," said the woman.

"The other night I seen you walking Romeo when he had colic," said the man. "Round and round the yard, you and that old horse. I was moved by your dedication."

But finally the man got up from his chair in the corner and went to the edge of the stage.

"Why, hello, boys," he said.

"We got a flat tire," said the actor playing the youngest brother, who was said to have been the mastermind of the outfit. "Wondering could we fix it here. Won't take but four–five hours."

"I don't know what kind of tires you have on that car, but it generally don't take that long," said the man. "Nor does it require guns to do it."

Bank Robbery Days drew business away from the lake and into town, so the Jack of Diamonds had a skeleton crew that night.

Keith Lyon was scrubbing the kitchen with a power buffer and Charlotte Blonde stood behind the bar playing Nim on napkins with the vacuum-cleaner dealer, Larry Rudd.

"I have you again," said Rudd. "You don't see it, do you?"

Charlotte studied the napkin with a pencil in her hand. "I don't," she said.

Just then three men came in and stood at the corner of the bar.

"We're not serving tables tonight," said Charlotte. "But you can sit anywhere and order here, and if you're hungry you can have something from the appetizer menu."

"Well, that sounds pretty good but we'll pass," said one of the men. He had thick shoulders and a round face and wore a fishing coat with pockets and straps and a Newfoundland and Labrador salmon badge. "Is Pierre around?"

"No," said Charlotte. "He's off tonight."

"That's disappointing," he said. "I'm his cousin Bobby. Maybe you might have heard him talk about me."

"Not that I recall."

"Do you know where I might find him? I'm just passing through this one night, and I'd feel bad if I didn't stop and see him."

"You ought to check over to the play," said Rudd.

"No," said Charlotte.

"What play is that?"

Charlotte jabbed Rudd in the hand with the pencil. "I'm afraid Pierre is out of town," she said.

Larry Rudd massaged his hand and looked at Charlotte uncertainly, but he loved knowing things and telling them too much to be silent. "Well, he used to go to it. I know he has gone."

"Maybe we'll take a swing by," said the one who called himself Pierre's cousin.

"Just go into town," said Rudd, "which is south out of here, or take a right. Now, that's not where it is, but you'll see the signs directing you to it. It's a big production."

An older man with the first man nodded his head solemnly with red furrowed brows. "Yeah, we saw the signs," he said.

"You're wasting your time," said Charlotte. "Pierre's not around."

"Well, who knows?" said the man in the fishing coat. "Maybe we'll like the play."

"What in hell you stab me for?" said Rudd when they had gone.

Charlotte went into the kitchen where the power buffer whined. Keith turned it off and pushed his safety goggles up on his forehead.

"Where's Pierre?" Charlotte said. "Did he go to the play?"

"He might have. Why?"

"Well, some guys were just in here looking for him. One said he was his cousin."

"His cousin. That sounds like a line, doesn't it. You didn't tell him anything, I hope."

"No, I didn't, but of course Larry Rudd had to be sitting there like their long-lost friend and he goes, 'Try the play, Pierre always goes to the play.' Is that true?"

"Fuck if I know."

Keith took off the goggles and set them beside the buffer on the shining silver table. He went out the side door and Charlotte followed him, and they looked around the parking lot, but the men were gone and there were just the cars that had been there before.

"All right, let me think," said Keith.

Meanwhile, the end of the play was drawing near. The farmer and the young bank robber played their fabled chess game in the living room of the stage.

"You're going to lose your knight to a pawn in three moves," said the robber. "I want you to know that. You folks don't have an accordion, do you? I play an awful good accordion."

"No," said the farmer. "No accordion."

The woman sat in a rocking chair reading *Wallace's Farmer*. The second brother paced at the back of the stage and the third stood looking absently out at the audience as if through a window.

"I think I left my coat at the bank," he said.

"Well, I tell you what," said his chess-playing brother. "We get out of here, you can buy a coat like you've never seen."

"There was tear gas on it. I threw it down and stepped on it."

"You can buy a whole coat *store*."

"I think my name was on it."

"You what?"

"Written inside the collar."

"Ohh, he does not like that," said the farmer.

The young robber got up from the chessboard and cleared it with a violent sweep of his arm. Chessmen clattered every which way and bounced off the stage.

"My beautiful plan," he said. "All cut to ribbons."

"It's only justice," said the woman from her rocker. "It catches up with the least of us."

"I have heard that," said the robber. "But it makes it sound like you'll have a little time before it does. Not that you will hand justice a coat with your name on it on the way out the door."

Carrie straightened curiously and looked at Pierre and reached into her pocket. It was her phone.

"Hello," she said quietly. "Yeah. We're in the middle of the play.... Okay. Just a minute."

She handed the phone to Pierre. "It's for you. It's Keith Lyon."

NINE

Pierre left the play to take the call. He walked down the aisle and out of the machine shed and stood in the driveway with the little phone held to his ear.

"Uh-huh, uh-huh," he said. Then he went back into the shed and stood at the bar listening to Keith on the phone.

"Got it," he said. "I will."

He motioned for the man behind the table to pour some whiskey in a shot glass. He said goodbye, and folded the phone, and it snapped shut like the mouth of a small silver animal.

The whiskey was three dollars and he put the phone down and paid with a five. Pierre forgot about the phone and went outside and drank the whiskey, which tasted good.

Shane came walking up between the cars in the dark. He carried the sandy rock that had knocked him out.

Pierre knew what it was. They stood looking at each other for quite some time.

"You forgot this," said Shane.

"Keep it," said Pierre.

"That was by the way the stupidest possible thing you could have done."

"Go away," said Pierre. "Or later you'll say, 'I wish I had gone away.'"

"Do you have my money?"

"Not with me."

"Where is it?"

"I buried it."

"Then you will dig it up and give it back."

"Why would I?"

"Because I'll kill you. And if they come to help you I will kill them too. So everyone will know you had to drag some down with you. They won't even like you when you're dead."

They walked away from the shed.

"You lost," said Pierre. "You made the rules and you lost, and now you don't think you like the rules so much."

"Yeah, but by the same token, who the fuck asked you?" said Shane.

"When you stole my pack, you were saying that anything yours or mine would go to whoever could get away with it."

"What are you, a lawyer?" Shane hit Pierre in the head with the rock. "How you like that, lawyer man? It hurts, doesn't it?"

Pierre stumbled but he neither fell nor made a sound. There were two men smoking by the car.

"This the guy?" said the older one.

"Yeah," said Shane. "Says he buried the money."

"You believe him?"

"Well, it ain't at his place. We know that."

The man scratched his elbow and cleared his throat. "It doesn't sound right to me," he said. "People don't bury money anymore."

"Well, he says he did, Ned," said Shane. "If he's lying we'll find out soon enough."

"You went in my apartment," said Pierre.

"Yeah, we did," said Shane. "Those are some nice model boats, too, but I have to say you're like a fucking child. And they didn't hold up too well when we leaned on them."

"Now that was wrong," said Pierre.

"Shut up and get your dead ass in the car."

Shane took a kick at Pierre, but Pierre turned aside and caught his leg and threw him to the ground as he had learned to do.

"Well, this is going badly," said Ned. He hit Pierre in the neck with his fist. Pierre worked his jaw, trying to untangle the cords.

Shane stood up and brushed himself off with one hand while holding a gun in the other and backing Pierre down with the gun hand.

"The big violin too," he said. "Because Lyle thought the money might be in that. And I said how could it get in there. But then I thought why stand around arguing about it when we can just crush the motherfucker and we'll know. Now tell me where my money is."

"In an orchard," said Pierre.

They went along the road from the farm and they could see a line of cop cars coming down from the ridge in a curve of blue light.

Shane drove and Lyle and Ned were in the back with Pierre between them. The clouds had moved off and the moon was three-quarters full and riding low above the hills.

The turn signal clicked with its long-suffering sound as Shane waited to go left and the police cars shuddered by with lights but no sirens.

"They called them at the bar, I bet," said Shane.

"Police are never on time," said Lyle. "You notice that? They always get somewhere after something has happened but never while it's happening."

"Well, sometimes they do," said Ned. "Then it's a standoff and they get down behind the cruisers and talk into bullhorns."

"Rarely," said Lyle. "Very rarely."

"Did he tell you what this is about?" said Pierre. "He tried to steal my clothes and some paper plates and for that he lost seventy-seven thousand dollars."

"How much?" said Ned.

"Well, the amount doesn't matter," said Shane. "It's the idea that counts."

"You didn't say it was that much," said Lyle.

"You believe this thief over me?" said Shane. "I don't know what to say."

"We'll count it again once we have it," said Ned.

"Why?"

"Our fee is based on a percentage."

"Who said so?"

"You."

"That is what you said, Shane," said Lyle.

Shane was quiet driving along the road. Then he said, "You want to count it, be my guest."

"Good."

"You can count it, and *you* can recount it, and then you can count it together like smart young ladies in a bank."

"Yeah, we might do that."

"I don't care. It's my money. I can afford to be generous. But you're curious. I get that."

They stayed on the back roads. Ned didn't like relying on Pierre's directions, but in truth Pierre had no intention of leading them anywhere but the orchard. They could see the lights of Shale off to the south. Pierre tried to imagine that he would never see the town again but he couldn't really believe it.

They entered the orchard road at the place where Charlotte and Pierre had come out of the forest when Tim Geer was lost, or said to be anyway.

The headlights slid over the channeled bark of the trees and the front bumper bent the bleached grass that filled the roadbed. Pierre had driven the road several times so the tire tracks were easy to follow. The grass pressed against the chassis, seeming to float the car with a soft whispering sound like water.

Whenever Shane got up any speed at all he would have to slow and turn the wheel as the road wound its way up into the hills. It was a pretty quiet ride. Nobody had much to say in the presence of the creepy woods. Ned crossed and recrossed his arms as big men do and Lyle kept turning and looking out the back window to make sure no one was following.

"Of all the fucking places to put money," said Ned. "Did you ever hear of a safe-deposit box?"

"No, I never did."

"How'd you bring it up here?"

"In a car."

"And dug a hole."

"Yeah, what else."

"How'd you know somebody wouldn't find it?"

"Or an animal," said Lyle. "If it smelled the scent of humans."

Pierre was thinking it should have happened by now. He was trying to remember where exactly it had been and he wished that they would be quiet and allow him to concentrate.

"I don't know they wouldn't," he said.

"I want you to understand something," said Ned. "I think you're a liar. If that money isn't here, and I don't care why, you're going to be a very sorry son of a bitch. If the hole is empty, or you can't find the spot, or it was here yesterday, or possums rose up and ate the money, I don't care, because in that case I myself will—"

Then the car hit the chain across the road. Shane was going no more than twenty miles an hour, but that is too fast a speed at which to hit a chain. Maybe it would have been enough if the car had simply slammed to a halt, but what happened was more destructive. The chain came shrieking and bladelike up the hood, shattering the windshield and pushing in the corner posts of the roof so that rather than simply stopping the car the chain seemed to act as a giant hand that was grinding it into the road.

Then there were simultaneous detonations as the chain broke and the airbags went off. All of this happened in an instant, during which the car's interior filled with smoke and a blizzard of safety glass, and it was not difficult for Pierre, who was the only one who had any idea what was happening, to crawl across Lyle, open the door, and fall on the ground.

Tim Geer and Stella were walking among mannequins in an empty dress store in Rainville. The store had gone out of business and Tim had a key for reasons he did not explain.

"See anything you like?"

Stella felt the fabric of a wine-red dress with white roses. "This one isn't bad," she said.

Tim unzipped the dress and tried to lift it from the mannequin but the mannequin fell over and one of the arms came off.

"I'm having a hell of a time," he said.

"Just leave it, Tim."

"Say, about this business with Pierre."

"Yeah?"

"It is tonight."

"It is."

He nodded and set the mannequin back on its stand. "I kind of lied on that one."

"Why?"

"So you would stay out of it."

"I said I would."

"It is what it is."

"Does he live?"

"I don't know. I can see it going either way. But remember how you met him."

Tim Geer went behind the counter and turned off the lights in the store.

"This has all been extra time for him," he said.

Pierre ran down the road to the orchard where the night sky spread over the low trees, and the stars and moon were out, and he felt like he had arrived in his place. He turned to look back. The car moved very slowly and one headlight was still working, though pointing at the ground.

He went into the orchard shack and took his shotgun down from the rafters. The shells were in a box in the drawer of the table. He turned the gun over in his hands and loaded it with five shells and put a dozen into his pockets and he thought that if this were not enough it wouldn't matter how many more he had.

Pierre figured they might be close to giving it up. Shane might resist but his friends had little stake in the money and in fact would probably pay at this point just to go back to wherever they came from. And Shane himself would have got the worst of it when the car hit the chain. Twice now Pierre had got him to run his vehicle into something. Not one of the three seemed the picture of competence.

Pierre went to the window of the shed and cleaned the pane with the sleeve of his coat. The car waited with the one headlamp on and they were out of it and walking up the road. They had a flashlight and were shining it in the trees, making the shadows of branches lengthen and wheel.

Now Pierre wanted to do something before they got any closer. He wanted to fire the gun so they would know he had it. Maybe this would be the thing that would send them off. Of course he himself could run. Probably he could get down the way he and Charlotte Blonde had come up. There wasn't really a path but he could skid through the trees where they would never follow.

But then what?

No, he thought. He liked it up here. He'd got to this ground he knew and did not want to go back into the woods.

So he stepped out of the shed and aimed the gun at nothing and pulled the trigger.

He had never fired a gun in the dark and was surprised by the yellow flame. Then he kicked out the shell and moved off into the apple trees before they or he would have time to consider what they would do in response.

Shane and Ned and Lyle walked toward the shed shooting like gunfighters in the Old West. Glass broke and boards splintered. This was something to do but ineffectual because after the gun fired they had seen Pierre run off.

They stood on the boards outside the shed. Lyle looked around with the flashlight.

"You know, I've seen this movie," said Ned. "The outnumbered guy kills everybody."

"Lyle, go around."

"Around what?"

"The building."

"What do you mean?"

Shane grabbed him by the face. "Goddamn it. Go down one side, across the back, and come up the other side."

Lyle pushed Shane's hand away. "Why would I do that?"

"To see if he's there."

"He ran. I saw him."

"Just do what I ask."

"I don't want to. This is no good, Shane. I feel completely misled. And not just on the money."

"So he happens to have a gun. Does this make you afraid?"

"It isn't a question of fear," said Lyle. "It's a question of being told one thing and finding that, once you get out there, it's actually something else."

"I'm not going to stand here and compare notes with

you," said Shane. "If you're unable to walk around a simple goddamned shack in the dark, I will."

"No, I'll do it," said Lyle. "But I just want you to know that this whole operation is a lot of shit."

"Good. Give me the flashlight."

"No."

"Think. What is a flashlight but a big bright target. Think, Lyle."

Lyle gave Shane the light and left and Shane and Ned went inside the shed, walking on the broken glass.

Shane shone the flashlight in the cobwebbed corners of the little building. "This guy is fucking pissing me off," he said.

"You think the money's here?"

"Unlikely. Seems like he had it pretty well thought out."

"So let's leave."

"The car's all mangled."

"It's insured," said Ned. "We'll ditch it and get another one."

"You go. I won't be able to hold my head up in a crowd if I go back now."

They heard footsteps on the boards and then Lyle looked in the door. "He ain't around," he said.

Shane walked to the doorway. "Of course he ain't," he said. "You know why?"

"Because he took off."

"And who let him?"

"What was I supposed to do?"

"Well, I'm glad you asked that," said Shane. "First, a guy walks all over you getting out of a car you're trying to keep him *in,* and you have a gun, you stop him. That's one big item that should be on your checklist. Here, let me show you. You take the gun in this hand. Just like this here. And then you say, you know, whatever comes to mind. Don't move. Hold it right there. Stop or I'll shoot. And if he doesn't, then you make sure he does."

Lyle laughed. "Jesus Christ, you've got to be kidding me," he said. "I thought you were pretty low but I had no idea of this. You ran your car into a chain. You did that. And now you're trying to put it on me? That's why he got away. Because he told you to drive into a chain and you, like a dumb fuck, did it. Do you believe this, Ned? Do you believe this lowlife?"

"Yeah, cut it out," said Ned. "Nobody stopped him, not just Lyle."

Shane brought the gun up and pulled the trigger and Lyle fell off the porch and lay in the grass.

"Now I have seen it all," said Ned.

"Fucking Shane shot me," said Lyle.

"Oh, you're not hurt," said Shane. "Keep it down."

"Not hurt? You shot him in the heart," said Ned.

"Well, you push me and you push me and I don't know what you think is going to happen."

"This is awful," said Lyle. "Now I'm going to die in some demented nature preserve, or I don't even know what it is, that you brought us to because you could not hold on to your own money."

"You're not going to die," said Ned. "We'll take you somewhere and get you fixed up."

"How?" said Lyle. "*The car is wrecked to shit.*"

"We'll go slow."

"Give my money to my sister."

"What money is that?"

"When we get the money off this kid. My cut goes to my sister. Count it and give her my share, Ned. She works at that copy place. You know. Where you take your résumé. And I have a passbook. It's not a lot. I think there's a thousand bucks. I don't really know. I think it's in the drawer. Whatever it says. Or if your dog is lost. And you go out with a staple gun. You know her, don't you?"

"Yeah, Lyle, I'll get it to her."

"Her name is Laurie. Give her my money. There's just kind of a hesitance there. I really like people. But I don't know how it will end. Ned, step on my hand, will you?"

"Why?"

"To hold it down."

"No, I'm not going to do that."

"Do you believe this?"

"Just stay quiet."

Lyle didn't last much longer. He died there on the grass. Ned sat down on the edge of the porch and picked up the shell from Pierre's gun. It was still warm and smelled like a day of hunting.

"Well, I don't know what to say," said Ned. "I believe I will be going."

"That's okay. I do the work. It's like that house. I did the work. I killed the people. You just kind of handle the phones."

Ned stood and brushed off his pant legs. "Lyle was right about you. Now he's dead and some kid who you tried to rip off probably has a bead on us as we speak. It's a twelve-gauge, by the way."

"You taking the car?" said Shane.

"I don't know. I guess I'll give it a try."

"Yeah, that'll probably work."

"Don't come back to my place. I'll put your stuff in a box and mail it wherever you want."

"I'll call you sometime."

Shane knelt, unlacing his boot and staring at the still face of Lyle.

"What are you doing that for?" said Ned.

"They hurt my feet."

Pierre walked back in the orchard and sat down cross-legged at the base of an old willow where the bark fanned out, making something like a chair. It wasn't as uncomfortable as you would think. Kind of cold, though. He took his leather gloves out of his pocket and put them on.

He stayed in that place a long time. He heard the shot that was fired and wondered if Ned and Lyle had turned on Shane and killed him. That would mean Pierre's part was over. Sometime later he saw the light of the car as it made a laborious three-point turn and limped from the orchard. That could be them leaving. Maybe this was too optimistic. But someone was leaving. He wondered how far they could possibly get in such a car.

He lowered his head and nodded off. When he woke he looked at his watch. He had slept for twenty minutes. Now there was another light, nearer, not on the road, maybe forty yards up and two or three rows over. That would be the flashlight. It turned in slow circles. It didn't go anywhere. Pierre watched the light and its monotonous turning for half an hour. If anyone was holding it there was something wrong with him.

He knew how to walk in the woods without making noise. It was all in planting the heels and keeping your weight back until you knew you there was nothing that would snap. But it took a long time.

No one held the flashlight. It turned in midair beneath the branches of an apple tree. Pierre reached up and found that the light had been suspended by a string and turned it off.

Isn't that strange, he thought. But now I know.

He turned in time to see the sparks in the trees across the way. Then came the sound. He brought the old Savage gun up and fired, and the kick knocked him down.

A branch cracked and a dark shape fell to the ground like a night bird.

He felt something like a wire in the side of his throat or maybe the blade of a band saw, bright and cold. He brought his hand up and touched the hole that had been made.

What did I care what that light was, he thought.

Above him he saw the moon shining in the blue arms of the branches.

Stella found the first one dead in front of the cabin and the second dying under a tree. She put her hand behind his head and raised it up.

"Did you burn Leslie's house?" she said.

"You don't have anything to drink, do you?"

"No. Tell me. Did you do it?"

"It wasn't hers. I didn't know."

"But you did."

"Yeah."

"Who helped you?"

"No one."

"Then why did you do it?"

"Ned hired me."

"And where would he be?"

"Who are you?"

"I'm Pierre's friend."

"Oh, fuck, of course. You would be."

"Where's the one who hired you?"

"You're all full of light."

"Don't look at me."

"He left in the car."

"And Pierre."

"I don't know, around here somewhere."

"Did he kill you?"

"Yeah, probably. Very soon I think you will be able to say that."

"I think I can say it now," said Stella.

Pierre was the last one she found. The grass was dark and glistening beneath his head.

"Oh," she said. "Oh, damn."

She fell to her knees and took him by the shoulders and pulled him to her. And there she held him until the light began to come up in the orchard.

TEN

TELEGRAM SAM the state policeman came up at dawn on Sunday morning and ran yellow tape from tree to tree across the road where it opened into the orchard. He unfolded plastic sawhorses and arranged them in a line and went back to his cruiser and took a tape measure from the glove box.

A sheriff's deputy walked up with coffee in a Styrofoam cup. "They're all three here," he said.

"And dead," said the trooper.

"Yes, sir."

"Edmund Anderson said one, when he left."

The deputy poured the coffee on the ground and shook the cup out. "Well, there's three now."

"Pierre Hunter?"

The deputy nodded. "According to his license."

"Shane Hall."

"And some other guy."

"Do you have a camera?"

"I was just getting it."

"You know I maybe could've stopped this."

"How?"

"I'd heard things. About this Hall, and him looking for Hunter."

"Well, you heard it, sure."

"We all did."

"I didn't. I don't even know who they are. But my point is, you hear a lot of things."

"I agree with that."

"I probably hear about ten things a day that I could look back at any one of them after the fact and say, 'Oh, sure.' But I don't know which ones, versus the vast majority of stuff that's just nothing."

"Well, you don't know."

"Of course you don't."

"I did talk to him, though."

"Hunter."

"Yeah. Tried to get it out of him—what was going on."

"You can't help those who will not help themselves. What'd the guy have it in for him about?"

"Oh, some deal. You know. Chance encounter. Unresolved incident from the highway."

"Well," said the deputy, "it would seem to be resolved now anyway."

The reporters began arriving in the bright morning and they stood shifting their legs like eager horses at the boundary of tape. They looked with longing into the gnarled gray trees where the bodies were.

"All right," said Telegram Sam. "We will start. And you will have to be patient. There's a lot we don't know."

The Reverend John Morris woke up that morning and got out of bed at the parsonage and showered and shaved and got dressed and sat in the kitchen eating toast and listening to the news on the radio.

At first they said only that some people had been killed and then a little later while he was washing the dishes they broke in on the music to give the names.

He sat down again and smoked a cigarette. He had a flimsy red metal ashtray with fluted edges that kept sliding away from him on the table. So he laid the burning cigarette on the linoleum, got his toolbox from under the sink, and nailed the ashtray to the table, and the ashes bounced all over the place as he hammered.

He picked up the cigarette and ground it out in the immovable ashtray. In a time like this he knew it was customary for a minister to say something profound to the people. And a good minister would do that, he thought: ditch the sermon and come up with something deep and moving—all the more moving most likely for its spontaneous quality.

And God love the ones who can pull that off, but I am not among them, he thought. You'd have to be calm and wise, and look at me; here I've driven a nail into a perfectly good table.

In the afternoon he went to the Jack of Diamonds. It was closed and Keith Lyon and Charlotte Blonde were hanging a black sash across the front below the windows. The pastor helped them, gathering the cloth and holding it off the ground as they worked.

Then they stood back by the road and saw that it looked all right and somber and they went into the tavern, where they sat at a table and drank Ouzo from heavy octagonal glasses that bent the light, and they hardly spoke, because there was nothing to say.

Pierre and Stella walked along the road arm in arm. The dirt was soft and gray and the shadows of the leaves made dark patterns on the ground. They could hear the sound of a stream ahead. Moss colored the stones and elaborate mushrooms sprouted from the bark.

"And then what?" said Pierre.

"You go down them," she said.

"Down the stairs."

"Right. And you walk for a long way, and then you come to a room."

"At the bottom of the stairs."

"No. You go down the stairs and then you walk for a long way. To a room, with a light and a bed."

"Like a motel."

"Yeah, kind of. Like a hotel."

"Oh, come on."

"No, that's what it is. So you will know it. And you lie down. Which you'll want to do because you'll be very tired. And so you go to sleep. And what you dream becomes your new life."

"Will I remember this?"

"Probably not. Most people don't. But I will. And I'll find you. I promise."

"Maybe I'll remember."

"When I see you again you will. Maybe not all of it. But enough."

They crossed a low stone wall and walked down to the stream they'd been hearing. There was a small island in the center with the water crashing around it, and a fallen evergreen formed a bridge from the bank. They walked across, holding their arms out for balance. In the center of the little island white boulders framed a slanted green door like that of a storm cellar.

The sign on the door said:

THIS DOOR IS

TO BE KEPT CLOSED

AT ALL TIMES

NO EXCEPTIONS

"This is it," said Pierre.

"I can't go with you."

"Really."

She put her arms around him and kissed him. "I'm sorry, Pierre. I love you."

"Maybe you can go with me partway."

"I can't."

Pierre reached down and took hold of the brass handle of the door. "It's locked," he said.

"Use the key," she said.

He took the key from his pocket and turned it in the lock. Then he opened the door and let it down easy on the white rocks. Stone stairs went down into the darkness.

"Well, they probably couldn't make this much scarier if they tried," he said.

"I know." She was crying.

"I would do it all the same," said Pierre.

He went down the stairs and she watched him go, and when she couldn't see him anymore she closed the door and sat down on the rocks. She stayed on the island through two nights of rain. Late on the third night she appeared at the Jack of Diamonds, where Charlotte Blonde gave her a change of clothes, and Keith fixed her supper, and Charlotte took her down to the storeroom and made up the pullout sofa for her to sleep on.

* * *

The rain stopped in time for Pierre's funeral. Musicians came down from Desmond City to play Edward Elgar's Cello Concerto in E Minor, which Pierre had once played in church. Allison Kennedy and the Carbon Family performed "When the Roses Bloom Again."

And John Morris gave the eulogy, part of which went like this:

"These are the days when we say 'at least,'" he said. "Perhaps you've heard this in yourself, or a remark that someone has made. 'At least Pierre was in love.' 'At least he got the men with the guns away from the crowded play.' 'At least his parents did not live to see what would happen.' That is one I find particularly strange, yet I have heard it. And this is what we do. We try to find a plan in operation, and when we don't find one, we make it up. Ladies and gentlemen, we make it up. This is not to say that there is no plan but only that we in our limited vision cannot see it. How could we? For we are inside a great and wondrous world that is more or less of a mystery even to those who think about it.

"One man passing through, another coming home. A random moment on the highway. A rental car that collides with a chain in the dark of the woods. Where was this body in relationship to that body. Scraps and maps and rumors in the newspaper. We say that we owe it to Pierre's memory to know the smallest detail. But I must say I don't believe it. What happened in that place can't be known and it can't be undone, as much as we would have it otherwise.

"What may be in our power to undo, however, is our tragic avoidance of the brevity of life," said the Reverend Morris. "A friend of Pierre's told me that in one of their last conversations he expressed the opinion that living is 'fun.' 'How do you mean?' she asked him. His answer came in three parts, which I would characterize as art, love, and nature. More specifically, Pierre said he found it fun 'when leaves move.' Now we may take this as an offhand remark, even meaningless, but maybe there is something to it. Perhaps what he meant is that this planet and these lives that we have been given are opportunities we do not comprehend. And so we misuse them, day by day. I expect he was only finding that out himself and wanted to tell someone. We look around in space and what do we see? Nothing. No leaves, no life, for who knows how far. And here we are. Are we doing the best we can for each other? For ourselves? Or can we find it in us to be more than we have been?"

It was after the eulogy that the trio from Desmond City played the Elgar song. The music rose like thunderclouds, gathering and breaking open in a storm on the lake.

One afternoon, Keith Lyon was sitting and smoking on a bench in the sun when a red-haired woman drove into the parking lot of the Jack of Diamonds and got out of her car wearing a tan suit with green stitching on the lapels.

"We're not open till five-thirty," he said.

"That's okay," she said. "I'm here about Pierre Hunter."

"Well," said Keith.

"I know," she said. "I called his apartment the other night and the landlord answered the phone. He told me what happened. Said the place was left a terrible mess."

"It was, too," said Keith. "I've got to get over there."

"I met him in the summer," she said. "I live in Utah and he was going through town and we spent the night together. Then later he sent me some money in a box."

"So that was you."

"Well, I've wanted to talk to him for a while. The hotel had a record but they couldn't find it."

"Are you hungry? Can I make you an omelet or something?"

"No, that's all right," she said. "Maybe you could just tell me how to get to the cemetery. I have some flowers I want to lay down."

"I'll take you there," said Keith.

"My name is Linda," she said.

They got in the car and drove down to South Cemetery. It was a warm afternoon and the trees had turned colors all along the hills. Keith felt he might fall asleep in the warmth of the car. He had been very tired lately.

They came to the cemetery, which was high and isolated with a valley reaching out to the west, and they walked out through the stones to a bank of black dirt.

Keith wondered if there was such a thing as a spirit that went on and he doubted it but at the same time wanted to think there might be.

The woman from Utah knelt before the grave and put down the orange lilies she had brought.

"I never got to thank you," she said. "So ... you know, thanks. But I couldn't go through with it."

She turned to Keith, who was standing with his arms folded in the sun.

"I couldn't," she said. "I have the money in the car."

"Go through with what?"

"Oh, okay. I had told Pierre I might have plastic surgery someday. You know, just casually. And we said it would be expensive. So then two weeks later all this money comes."

"Don't tell me if you don't want to, but—"

"For the scars," she said. "On my face. Don't you see them?"

Keith held his hand out to her and she took it and got up.

"Well, a little bit I do," he said.

"I talked to some doctors and they said they could maybe reduce them a little but they couldn't take them away entirely. It's much less of a sure thing than Pierre and I thought. So I figured if I'm going to have scars anyway I might as well have the ones I made."

"They're really not that bad."

"Thank you," she said. "Anyway, I have the money. Maybe it should go to his estate."

"I don't think he has one."

"Or family."

Keith shook his head. "His mother and father are right here."

"Can I ask you something?"

"Sure."

"Did the money have to do with what happened?"

"Yeah, it did. But you shouldn't feel bad. I think he would have done that no matter what."

"I don't feel bad. But strange, I guess. I don't know how to feel."

"There's a lot of that," said Keith.

They drove from the cemetery back to the Jack of Diamonds. Keith opened the door to get out but said, "The more I think about it, keep the money. He gave it to you. He never told me for what. I think he wanted you to do whatever you wanted."

"Let me think about that."

"Just keep it."

On the next day Linda met Keith at Pierre's apartment in Shale. It was ransacked as bad as anything either of them had seen.

"See what they did," he said.

Everything that could have hidden money and a lot that couldn't have was gutted or smashed or torn or kicked in or knocked over. It was a universe of shards, shreds, and splinters. You could hardly see floor anywhere.

He traced a flat gray cord from the wall and fished the telephone from the debris and dialed to order a Dumpster. As he waited to talk to someone, he brushed his free hand on his pants and looked at it.

"There's this silver dust all over everything," he said.

Keith had brought push brooms and a flat-blade snow shovel and they spent most of the day pushing everything down the length of the apartment and onto the back porch, from which it could be dropped two stories to the Dumpster in the alley. It did not take long for them to see that it would take more than one day.

Around five o'clock Keith's back began to hurt and he went down the hall and into the bathroom to look for an aspirin. When he opened the medicine cabinet he found this note taped inside the door:

silver dollar to Charlotte Blonde
guns to Roland Miles
MGA to Carrie Sloan
gray felt hat to Keith Lyon
ice skates to Stella Rosmarin

Keith called for Linda and she joined him in the bathroom and stood there reading the note.

"We should look for these things," he said.

"These five get the money," she said. "Divide it up equal."

"I don't want it."

"Then give it away. You said I should do what I want with it and that's what I want."

She left the bathroom and Keith took an Advil and cupped his hand under the faucet for the water. When he went back into the kitchen he saw that she had found the gray felt hat and was wearing it.

Roland and Carrie Miles sat at the end of a pier on an island off the western coast of Florida. They were on vacation and it would be cold back home. The pier was long and at the end rose a square building with a bait shop below and restaurant above.

Roland was smoking and fishing and Carrie leaned back on her arms with her face turned to the sun. The water moved past in silver swells that went on and turned to foam on a white beach lined with little houses.

"We should move here," she said.

Roland reeled in an empty hook and put a shrimp on it and cast it back under the dock. There was supposed to be a barracuda that lurked there, appearing every once in a while to steal a fish off a line.

"All right," he said. "You find a place and I'll bring our stuff down in a yellow truck."

"We could wear sandals and have a fire on the beach at night."

"Come on, you old legendary barracuda."

"And you'd come home at night with fish in a bucket and I'd say, 'What did you catch, my love?'"

"Find a place with French doors."

"And I would say, 'Look, darling, look what I found. It's a sand dollar.'"

Roland flicked the rod and spun the reel and the hook danced up clean and jangling. "The bastard took my bait again."

"And we would never fight. Because it's too hot and we would be in tune with the rhythm of life."

He got up and handed her the rod and reel. "Here, you try for a while," he said. "Do you want a beer?"

"Sure."

She baited the hook and looped another sinker on

the line and cast far out into the ocean, away from the pier, thinking she would show him how it's done.

They were renting a cottage on the beach on the other side of the island. That night Roland wanted to walk to a bar down the road and Carrie told him to go ahead as she felt like staying in.

She sat out on the patio and wrote by the light of an orange lamp on the table.

> *Bank Robbery Days won't come again,*
> *Which this year came too true:*
> *The killings three I could not foresee*
> *When I gave the phone to you.*
> *It's cold and gray in Shale now*
> *And still I drive your car.*
> *The top is down, I shift the gears,*
> *I roam around with wind-dried tears*
> *And wonder where you are.*

Then she walked down the sand path to the Gulf of Mexico and waded into the water. On the horizon she could see three lighted ships like distant cities.

Out past the breaking waves she dove in and swam with eyes open in the dark sea, and she thought of the big night fishes cruising around in the deeps with eyes like saucers and fanning fins.

When the gulf changed temperature at the sand bar she let her feet drop down and stood with the water shoulder-high and turned and looked back at the shore. The cottage lights were like a village among the condo towers.

She pushed back her wet hair and waited there with her hands on top of her head and water beading on her face. Yes, she thought, they could live in this place. There might be good things to do here. And it wouldn't have to be forever.

It's a warm day late in the fall. Hunting in the hills, he finds an orchard he has never seen before, high and green in the afternoon sun. It is deserted; the trees are young and well tended. He's walked for miles and as he moves through the orchard he realizes all at once how tired he is. He sits down at the base of a willow tree, lays his gun beside him. His eyes close, his legs unfold, and he breathes deeply.

When he wakes it is dark and cool. The moon is overhead. He has no idea how long he has slept. It feels like days. A woman in a long coat and boots stands looking at him.

"Are you all right?" she says.

"I am," he says. "What time is it?"

"I don't know. Not too late."

"I must have fallen asleep."

"Yeah, I guess so. I'm walking into town if you're going that way."

He gets up and looks around. "I don't know what happened. I sat down to rest this afternoon and that's the last thing I know."

"It was a great day," she says. "And it's supposed to stay this way for a while."

"What brings you out here?"

She smiles. "Well, that's a good question."

He picks up the shotgun. He has the strangest feeling that he knows this place, knows this woman. He figures it's because he just woke up, that he's still partly dreaming. But when he takes her hand it feels warm and real, and they walk down the orchard row with the moonlight on the leaves.